DREAMING OF THE DEMON

A NOVELLA OF HIDDEN HOLLOW

HIDDEN HOLLOW
BOOK 1.5

EVANGELINE ANDERSON

AUTHOR'S NOTES

Author's Note #1—This short novel is not Hidden Hollow book 2, it's more like a fun little interlude between the main books in the series and it can be read as a STAND ALONE. It's not as long as my usual books, so I have priced it less than usual. I hope you enjoy reading it as much as I enjoyed writing it.

Author's Note #2—Because this book is shorter than my usual books, I am offering it for a lower price that my usual books.

What you'll get in this Spicy, Small Town Monster Romance:

- Spicy times with an actual plot
- Handsome Incubus who's eager to please and has a tail that stings in all the right places
- A Pilgrim orgy
- All kinds of Creatures including Centaurs, Krakens, Witches, Demons, Ogres and more…

To all the readers who gave me ideas for this little novella. I ultimately chose to go in a different direction, but I love brainstorming with you all! And to my dear friend Laura, who had the idea of a mysterious guy in a portrait coming to life in the first place and to the wonderful Kim who made us watch that boring movie that gave Laura the idea. Thanks for always being an inspiration in my life and writing, guys!

CHAPTER ONE

"Happy Birthday to me, Happy Birthday to me, Happy Birthday, dear Celia, Happy Birthday to me," I sang sadly under my breath before blowing out the candle on the Strawberry Supreme cupcake, which was my personal favorite and a best seller at the bakery I owned. Then I just sat there looking at it—I didn't even have the heart to take a bite.

I was turning forty and I was all alone—no husband, no kids, and no family at all besides one estranged brother I hadn't seen in years. I was officially in what my Great Aunt would have called a "blue funk."

"It wouldn't be so bad if I was at least *dating* someone," I muttered, as I pinched off a piece of my birthday cupcake. It was delicious as always, but that didn't lift my spirits. "I mean, I'd even settle for a hook-up at this point. Just a quick, one-night stand would work. At least it would be *something.*"

But it seemed like no one was interested in hooking up with a curvy, plus-sized bakery owner who was edging into middle age. Middle age—God!

I slapped the kitchen table and stood up, unable to stand sitting still anymore. I started pacing the black and white checked tiles of the roomy kitchen. It was my favorite space in the old, rambling Victorian house my Great Aunt Gertrude had left me in her will. She had left me her bakery, The Lost Lamb, too and I had been running it successfully for the past five years.

But running a successful small business means you have almost no time for yourself. And that goes double for owning a bakery—especially in a magical town like Hidden Hollow where Creatures with big appetites live side-by-side with the few human inhabitants.

I have to make quadruple batches of every recipe because your average Orc or Minotaur or Centaur will inhale a dozen donuts in two bites and then ask for more. And don't get me started on my hubcap-sized cinnamon rolls, my Frisbee-sized chocolate chip cookies, or my mountainous blueberry muffins—not to mention the enormous fifteen-layer Devil's Food cakes I make on Saturdays only because they take so much time and oven space.

But baking for supernatural beings—Creatures as they call themselves—is only part of living in Hidden Hollow. It's a special place —a small New England town located in the Berkshires Mountains.

A magical bubble around the town keeps non-magical folk out. It also keeps the outside world's weather at bay. Years ago the town council took a vote and everyone agreed that their favorite time of year was Fall—peak leaf season to be exact. So now it's almost always Autumn.

I say "almost" because there are a few exceptions. In May we have a whole month of Spring. In August it's Summer, and in December it's Winter with big, feathery snowflakes that collect in gorgeous drifts, but never on the road, because that would be inconvenient. Every other month of the year it's Autumn and except for the constant leaf raking— which most folks around here manage by magic—it's amazing.

Hidden Hollow is a beautiful place to live and I hadn't regretted moving here a bit…until now.

Now I had to wonder if I had done the right thing when I accepted my Great Aunt's invitation—which came in the form of a cryptic greeting card with a picture of a fresh baked loaf of bread on the outside and the words, *You are the Only One who can Help Me! Please Come— Love, Aunt Gertrude,* in her untidy scrawl inside.

At that point I'd had only a very vague notion of who my Great Aunt was. My Mom had mentioned something about her once—she had apparently disappeared mysteriously when she was in her thirties. She left an unhappy husband and a troubled marriage behind but no kids. In fact, according to my mother that was one reason Great Aunt Gertrude's marriage was so unhappy—she didn't want children and made no secret about it.

"She just never had any use for them," my mother said, shrugging. "After she disappeared, they tried to say that Great Uncle Lou killed her but they never found her body, so they couldn't make it stick. He moved out to California and married again and had three sons and two daughters, so I guess that made him happy."

"But what happened to Great Aunt Gertrude?" I asked, focused on the mystery that surrounded my long-lost relation.

My Mom shrugged.

"Nobody knows. It was strange too—she disappeared in the middle of the day and didn't take a thing with her. One minute she was in the kitchen making supper for Uncle Lou and the next minute she was gone. He said he smelled burning and ran in to see what was happening because Great Aunt Gertrude *never* burned anything. In fact, her cooking and baking were wonderful—he always said it was the only reason he stayed with her."

"So what *happened?*" I asked, impatient with the tangent she'd gone off on. "Where did she *go?*"

"Nobody knows, but she left a batch of her famous butter rolls in the oven to burn and didn't take a thing with her," Mom said. "Not a single piece of clothing—not even her purse or a sweater. She just vanished in the middle of a regular, ordinary day and she was never seen again." She sighed and got a sad look in her eyes. "It's a shame I didn't get some of her recipes before she went—she made the most mouthwatering pastries. I remember looking forward to her lemon cream tarts and her apple hand pies all year."

So that was all I knew about my Great Aunt Gertrude until I got the mysterious card in the mail. The minute I read it, I wished I could call my Mom—but she and my Dad were long gone by then. Dad died of lung cancer—he never could quit smoking—and my Mom just kind of faded away a year afterwards. They'd always been extremely close and though it didn't make any medical sense, I had the strong feeling that she'd died of a broken heart. That was the kind of love I was looking for…but I had never found it.

I have a younger brother, as I think I mentioned before, but we aren't close and there was nobody else to call. I sat there reading and re-reading the card and finally I said aloud,

"I'd help if I could, but she didn't even leave me an address or a phone number!"

At that point, it was like an invisible finger tipped in fire began drawing in the empty air in front of me. I stared in shock as it formed a door…a door which opened onto a beautiful Fall landscape even though it was blazing hot summer outside my own front door.

The minute I walked through the doorway—because of course I did —I was greeted by a little old lady with sparkling blue eyes, much like my own, and pure white hair done up in a fashionable twist at the back of her head.

"Oh, *there* you are!" she exclaimed, holding both hands out to me. "I'm so glad you agreed to come help!"

It was my Great Aunt Gertrude, of course. She had also received a magical invitation to Hidden Hollow, much like the one she'd sent to me. And since she wasn't happy in her marriage to Great Uncle Lou, "All that man wanted was food and sex and someone to clean up after him! I was tired of being his maid and his cook and his whore and not getting paid in anything but insults and complaints!" she said—she stepped through the doorway just as I had and found herself in Hidden Hollow.

Great Aunt Gertrude explained to me that only humans who have magic or Creatures—who are magic by their natures—are able to live within the magical bubble that protects the town. I protested, of course, that I had no magic at all.

"Nonsense!" she said briskly, frowning at me. "I've been watching you for ages—you never burn anything and everything you bake comes out perfectly. Doesn't it?"

"Er, well…I guess so," I admitted. I had never given this much thought before. It wasn't like I baked for a living back then, though I had always had a passion for it. I had a business degree and I was working at an accounting firm—a job that was duller than dirt but paid my bills and kept a roof over my head.

"Your bread dough always rises, your croissants are perfectly laminated, your pie dough is flakey, your biscuits are fluffy, and your cookies are just the right texture—a little crispy on the edges and chewy and gooey in the middle," Great Aunt Gertrude continued. "Right?"

"Right," I agreed. "But I don't see how being good at baking means I have magic."

"It means you're a Kitchen Witch!" my Great Aunt exclaimed. "Just like I am—just like our ancestors before us."

"I don't know," I said doubtfully. "My mom wasn't particularly good at baking or cooking. She *hated* making dinner—we got pizza and Chinese take-out more than any other kid I knew growing up."

My Great Aunt waved her hand impatiently.

"It skips a generation sometimes. I'm just glad *you* happened to get the talent, my dear, because I'm tired of working and I need someone to leave my bakery to."

"Your bakery?" I said blankly. "What bakery?"

"Why, The Lost Lamb, of course. I named it after myself, in a way," she said. "Since I was kind of like a poor lost lamb when I got here. I was called by the magic of Hidden Hollow just like I called you, but there was no family here to greet me when I came."

"Then who called you?" I asked, frowning.

"Oh, why, the Town Council of course. They decided that a bakery was needed and they did a magic finding spell for a Kitchen Witch of the right bloodline who would be capable of running it and who was unhappy enough in her regular life to leave everything and come here to stay." She spread her hands. "So, here I am! And here you are too—you wouldn't have answered my call if you had wanted to stay in the Mortal Realm."

"Um…" I thought of my boring job and the fact that I wasn't dating anyone and hadn't in almost a year. The dating apps are all trash —somehow they never come up with a decent man. (I think their algorithms do that on purpose to keep you hunting.) Anyway, all I had been getting were narcissists and gaslighters and Momma's boys who wanted me to do everything for them, including washing their underwear and packing their lunch every day, and I was frankly sick of it.

"Well?" Aunt Gertrude demanded again.

"What do you mean the Town Council wanted a Kitchen Witch 'of the right bloodline?'" I asked, playing for time. "What does that mean?"

"Oh, our family, the Hatches, have been witches from the beginning. In fact, one of our ancestors comes from here—though she got hung for her witchcraft during the Witch Trials, poor thing. That was Hester Hatch, our many times great grandmother," she explained. "But stick to the point—do you want to live here and run my bakery or not? I really want to travel some before I fade but I won't leave it to anyone outside the family. I need another Kitchen Witch with Hatch blood to run it—and you're the only one left."

I thought again of my dull job and non-existent love life and made a choice right then and there to stay in Hidden Hollow.

Great Aunt Gertrude stayed in town long enough to get me started —almost a whole year, in fact. She was patient with me and introduced me to everyone in town—many of whom weren't human. It took some time to get used to serving Centaurs and Orcs and Fairies and Pixies and all the rest, but I had been living in a big city with lots of diversity before I left and I enjoyed meeting new people so that helped.

My Great Aunt also advised me to get a familiar but I hadn't gotten around to that yet. She had a cat herself, named Nella that I swear was as smart as a person.

As a witch, you can choose any animal you want for your familiar —a dog or a cat are the most popular choices because they fit neatly into your life. You could choose a horse or a pig or a cow if you really wanted to but good luck getting them into the house at night. You can even have a raven or a parrot if you want one you can speak to. But Great Aunt Gertrude advised against that.

"Bird familiars tend to be extremely sarcastic and they scare customers off, being rude and swearing all the time," she told me. "A cat is wise and a dog is loyal. As a woman alone, you want a protector."

"Why—isn't it safe here?" I asked. Hidden Hollow seemed like such an idyllic little town—a place where no one even bothered to lock their doors at night and everybody knew everyone else.

But my Great Aunt gave me a dark look.

"It's as safe as it can be, but my house is located on the edge of the bubble," she said.

She went on to explain that the magical bubble that surrounded the town sometimes drew other Creatures—ones that weren't welcome in Hidden Hollow because of their evil tendencies. Social convention kept them out of the town itself—the Town Council would have them forcibly removed if necessary—but they could still get in around the edges of the town limits because they were technically magical creatures so the bubble didn't keep them out.

"You don't want to run in a Giant or a Troll, you know," Great Aunt Gertrude told me. "Or Goddess forbid an Ogre!"

"What's wrong with Ogres?" I asked, thinking of the lovable Shrek and his sidekick, Donkey.

"They're *horrible* Creatures—very bloodthirsty." Aunt Gertrude shivered. "They would look at you the same way you'd look at an especially ripe plum—something tasty to eat. Just another ingredient, you know. You *definitely* want to steer clear of them—having a dog as a familiar would help with that. A dog can bark to warn you if anyone is prowling around the house. I mean, I have it warded so they can't get in unless you let them in the front door, but you don't want to get caught unaware if there's an evil Creature lurking out there waiting to snatch you!"

Her words had scared me at first and I had been on my guard. But now, after five years of nothing more frightening than Chester the deaf Centaur stamping into the bakery and shouting loudly that he wanted three dozen double fudge brownies made with extra crispy hay—a common ingredient for Creatures who were part cow or horse—I had relaxed somewhat and my life had fallen into a pattern.

I got up extra early to take my morning walk and have some coffee and got to the bakery by five-thirty to start baking and prep work. We didn't open until eight—that gave me time to get several batches of cinnamon rolls, blueberry muffins, and almond croissants out. Once I turned the "closed" sign to "open" I was constantly back and forth between the register, the oven, and the workspace in the back, baking and helping customers while I worked on the other pastries and cookies the Lost Lamb was famous for.

I closed at five on the dot and spent the next few hours making dough for the next day and cleaning up—luckily my Great Aunt had given me a spell that handled most of the cleaning—and then I went home around seven, had dinner, and did it all again the next day.

It wasn't easy but I normally loved my routine. I had always enjoyed baking and thanks to the spells my Great Aunt had left me for cleaning and for multiplying basic ingredients—I had a doubling spell that I used at least fifty times a week—it was profitable as well. But the town had been growing lately—the magic bubble swelling to accommodate all the new magic users and Creatures who were moving away from the Mortal Realm where things were getting awfully crazy.

Lately things had gotten too busy for just one person alone to run

The Lost Lamb so I had hired some help—a Natural Witch called Sarah. She had moved to town after her Grandmother's will called to her and she was now living on the far side of Hidden Hollow.

Sarah had a bit of Kitchen Witch in her as well—she loved to bake and nurture people—so she was a perfect fit for The Lost Lamb. She'd been introduced to me by one of my regulars, an Orc called Rath, who had turned out to be her Heartmate.

I think it was seeing Sarah and Rath together that was making me so blue—that and the fact that I was turning forty. The two of them were so in love with each other you could practically smell it in the air when they got together. (It smelled like marzipan if you're wondering.)

Up until then, I hadn't missed having a man in my life. Like I said, the ones I kept matching with on the dating apps were all horrible and my daily routine was extremely busy. But when I opened my eyes on the morning of my fortieth birthday and realized that I was still single and I probably wasn't ever going to meet my own Heartmate, I began feeling blue. I had taken my birthday off to do something special…and now I realized that I had no one to do anything special with. It really sucked.

"It's not just Sarah and Rath," I muttered as I paced around the kitchen. "It's those damn dreams I keep having! What's wrong with me, anyway?"

The dreams had been coming steadily for the past six months—but the crazy thing was I couldn't remember them very well. I just woke up all hot and bothered with a sense of longing filling me. I would have chalked the whole thing up to perimenopause but Madam Healer, the town doctor who treated every one—both human and Creature—in Hidden Hollow, had given me magical herbs to fend it off.

Besides, the dreams left me with more than just hot flashes—I had a feeling like someone had been touching me and giving me pleasure, bringing me almost to the brink of coming right before I woke up and everything faded away—including my dream lover, whoever he might be.

"It's those damn dreams!" I muttered again, still pacing. "If I could just stop having them, I'm *sure* I'd be happy again. After all, I have a wonderful life! I own my own bakery, which is very successful. I have friends and a fulfilling career that I love—I mean it's *way* better than working in the accounting firm."

I stopped pacing and stood in front of the small mirror hanging on the kitchen's far wall. A full-figured woman with a plump but pretty face, big blue eyes, and long golden-brown hair stared back. Sure there were a few crow's feet forming at the corners of my eyes and there were laugh lines around my mouth but I hadn't found a single gray hair yet —probably because my hair was already a light color but so what? It still counted, right?

"I don't look half bad—for my age," I went on. Listing my attributes and successes was one way I cheered myself up when I was feeling down. Only this time it didn't seem to be helping. Nevertheless, I kept trying. "I'm a strong, beautiful, intelligent woman and I don't need a man or a Heartmate to be happy. I need to stop feeling sorry for myself!" I concluded, giving my reflection a stern look.

But it was easier said than done. No matter how I lectured myself, I still felt blue. Having finished my affirmation, I was about to sit down and pick at my birthday cupcake again, when the front doorbell rang.

I really wasn't in the mood for company. I was thinking of just ignoring the bell when I heard a familiar voice calling my name. Sighing, I turned to answer the door.

I had no idea what I was about to let into my house or how it was going to change my life forever...

CHAPTER TWO

"Celia? Are you in there? I know you must be because Sarah is running The Lost Lamb by herself. Come out here and hurry up—this thing is heavy!"

I hurried to the front door and jerked it open just in time to see Goody Albright standing there with one of the many Brownies she employed.

Brownies are magical beings who are kin to Fairies, though they're not nearly so pretty. They have brown, bark-like skin, knobbly knees and elbows, and long, crooked noses. They're extremely hard workers and I had been thinking of hiring one to work at The Lost Lamb, running the register, before Sarah had come along.

Goody Albright is also a witch—like most of the humans in town —and she owns The Red Lion, Hidden Hollow's stately old bed and breakfast. Today she was wearing one of her many brightly colored muumuus and had her curly gray hair tied up in a paisley kerchief. Her sharp green eyes were narrowed with effort behind her gold rimmed spectacles—possibly because she was holding one end of a perfectly enormous portrait. The Brownie was holding the other end and her skinny arms were trembling.

"For the Goddess's sake, let us in!" Goody Albright exclaimed. "This is so heavy we're bound to drop it if we don't put it down soon! And if that happens I'm just sure the frame will crack—it's positively ancient!"

I didn't think the frame—which was made of some heavy, dark wood—looked likely to crack even if you went after it with a sledgehammer, but I didn't want to be rude.

"Come in, come in," I said, standing to one side and holding the door open for them.

"Thank you!" With much huffing and puffing, Goody Albright and the Brownie lugged the enormous portrait into my living room and sat it on the foyer floor with a solid-sounding *thud.*

"What in the world is this and why did you bring it here?" I asked, looking at the portrait curiously.

It showed a very handsome man—no, not a man, I thought, looking at it again. He must be a Creature of some kind—he had horns and his skin had a reddish cast to it. Also, I thought I saw a tail curving around from behind him. Could he be a Demon of some kind?

He was dressed in a neatly tailored suit which looked somewhat old fashioned. It had a high collar and instead of a tie he was wearing a white lace cravat. There was a devilish glint in his black eyes—which held a hint of red, as though he had been staring into a fire when the artist painted him.

The strangest thing about the picture though, wasn't the subject—it was the fact that I felt like I had seen the Demon somewhere before. For some reason he looked extremely familiar to me. Maybe he resembled one of my customers? I had been seeing so many new faces in the bakery lately since the town was expanding…

"This, my dear, is your birthright," Goody Albright said importantly, dragging my attention away from the portrait.

"My what?" I said blankly, staring at her.

"Your birthright," she repeated impatiently. "Before your Great Aunt Gertrude left town, she instructed me to give it to you on your fortieth birthday—but only if you hadn't found your Heartmate yet."

"But she never said anything like that to me," I protested. "And why didn't she just give it to me herself back when I first came to Hidden Hollow?"

Goody Albright shrugged.

"I don't know. She didn't explain—she just instructed me to give it to you at the right time." She peered at me from over her gold rimmed spectacles. "You *haven't* found your Heartmate, have you?"

"No—it's just me, myself, and I." I shrugged. "I keep meaning to get a familiar but I don't have the time to train one right now."

"And it *is* your fortieth birthday—correct?" Goody Albright demanded.

"Yes," I said glumly. "Thanks for rubbing it in."

"Oh, Celia—I'm so sorry! I wasn't trying to rub anything in," she exclaimed, instantly contrite. "Besides, forty is just the *start* of a witch's life! Why, you could live almost indefinitely if you want to. Look at me—I'm over two hundred—not that a lady tells her age. And your Great Aunt Gertrude is still going strong—I just got a postcard from her all the way from Patagonia the other day and it sounds like she's really living it up. She's into armature paleontology now. Did you know they found the bones of one of the biggest dinosaurs ever discovered down there? It's called the 'Titanosaur' or something like that."

"I wish she would have come back to give me this thing—whatever it is—herself," I muttered, ignoring the tangent about dinosaurs. "I'm sorry, Goody Albright—I just miss her sometimes," I added, not wanting to sound rude.

"Of course you do, my dear." She patted my shoulder comfortingly. "Listen, don't read too much into this. I don't know why your Great Aunt wanted you to have it—maybe just because it's a valuable family heirloom. She said it's been in the Hatch family for *centuries*."

"Well, it's certainly interesting," I remarked, looking at the enormous portrait again. The man—or Demon—in it was nice to look at, even if he *did* have that mischievous look in his burning black eyes.

"Yes, it is." Goody Albright clapped her hands together briskly. "Now—where shall we hang it?"

"Er, hang it?" I asked uncertainly. The heavy dark wooden frame didn't match the decor of my house at all, which I tried to keep airy and light. I'd been thinking of just putting it up in the attic along with all the other junk—assuming I could get it up the stairs myself. But it was clear Goody Albright had other ideas.

"Yes, hang it," she said firmly. "Oh, I know just the place! Come on, Tilda!" she said to the Brownie.

The two of them hoisted the portrait again and marched out of the living area, down the hallway, around the corner, and right into my bedroom!

"Hey, I don't know about this!" I protested, trailing behind them. "I'm not sure I want it in here."

But Goody Albright was already taking down the nice, serene landscape I had on my bedroom wall and hoisting the strange Demon's portrait up in its place.

"I don't know about this," I said to her again. "I think I'll feel weird about him, uh, staring at me when I'm trying to go to sleep." Because the portrait was now directly opposite the large, four-poster oak bed where I slept every night.

"Nonsense, my dear—it's not like he can actually *see* you. It's just a picture, after all," Goody Albright said distractedly. No, Tilda—it's crooked. A little to the left, I think. There—perfect!" She stood back from the portrait, beaming in satisfaction. "Well, isn't that nice?"

I wasn't at all sure it was, but I could see there was nothing I could say to change her mind. Maybe I could just wait until she left and then take it down, I thought. Assuming I could handle it by myself—it really was huge and heavy.

I studied it again. The Demon in the portrait appeared to be life-sized or even bigger. If he was real, he would be nearly seven feet tall. Also, he had some serious muscles bulging the fabric of the old-fashioned suit. I was *sure* I'd never had a customer who looked like that —I would have remembered him. Why did he look so familiar?

"Well, my job is done here," Goody Albright remarked, dusting her hands together. "I'll see you later at Goldie's."

"Wait—what?" I said, frowning. Goldie's was the town's diner—a place where people and Creatures alike gathered for good home cooking. I supplied all their desserts.

Goody Albright sighed.

"All right, I hate to spoil the surprise, but we're having a birthday party for you, my dear. I'm only telling you because I can see you're in such a low mood you won't come otherwise," she added, giving me a sympathetic look. "It's at five sharp. Try to act surprised and don't give the game away when Sarah calls to invite you to have dinner with her and Rath. All right?"

"All right," I said, nodding. It did my wounded heart good to know my friends were planning a party for me. Not that I need to be the center of attention all the time—in fact, I mostly hate that. But it was nice to know I had people in my life who cared. See—who needs a man?

Not me, I decided as I waved Goody Albright and Tilda off at my front door. Having delivered my "birthright," Goody A was anxious to get back to the business of running The Red Lion. I didn't blame her. As a small business owner myself, I knew how hard it was to keep things running smoothly and how easily everything can go straight to hell if you're not careful.

Sighing, I shut the door behind them and went back to look at the portrait some more. Standing in front of it, I frowned uncertainly—had the Demon in the picture *moved* somehow? I could have sworn that his left hand was in his pocket before—now it was pressed over his heart showing long, artistic fingers with short, neat fingernails that appeared to be very clean. Which was nice—I can't stand a man with dirty fingernails. But still—had he moved?

"Well, I know one place you're moving, buddy," I told him. "You're moving on up to the attic where you can't freak me out at night."

But when I grabbed the frame and attempted to push it up so I could get it off the nail it was hanging on, it wouldn't budge. I tried again with the same result—it felt like the portrait of the Demon had been glued to the wall!

"What the hell is going on here?" I muttered. Giving up on pushing the portrait up or down, I tried instead to work my fingertips under the outer edge—with the same result. Nothing. The portrait was stuck fast to the wall and there was nothing I could do to loosen it.

I thought about trying to find a crowbar—but wouldn't that damage the wall? Also, I didn't think this was a problem with a physical solution. I could feel the tingling of magic in my fingertips when I touched the place where the heavy wooden frame and the wall were connected. I was going to have to ask a witch who had more power than me to get the damn thing down. Maybe I could get Sarah to come try her hand at it after the party tonight...

Deciding to put the problem off until later, I went to the bathroom to take a shower and get ready. I didn't want to look like a mess for my own surprise birthday party. No, I wasn't upset with Goody Albright for spoiling the surprise—I was glad to have some advance notice so I could look presentable. I don't like sudden surprises.

I had no idea I was in for a big one that night.

CHAPTER THREE

The party went well—Goldie's was packed with all my friends and regular customers. I was suitably "shocked" when I walk in and everyone shouted "Surprise!" I made my eyes wide and gasped, "Oh my God—you *guys!*" in a very convincing way, if I do say so myself.

Goody Albright seemed to agree.

"Very nice, my dear," she murmured in my ear as she hugged me. "If you ever get tired of baking you could have a whole second career in Hollywood!"

I laughed and hugged her back. I was about to ask her about the portrait and how to remove it, when Sarah swooped in and grabbed me for another hug.

"Happy Birthday, Celia!" she said, grinning from ear-to-ear. "I'm so glad I get to celebrate it with you!"

"Aww, thanks so much, hon," I said, hugging her back. Sarah is such a sweetheart—I might be a little jealous that she found her Heartmate literally on the first day she came to Hidden Hollow, but I could never be mad at her. Also, she's another curvy girl, like me so seeing her with a hot, muscular Orc like Rath gave me hope that I might still find someone myself.

The party was a smash and people kept coming in. Somehow they all fit, though normally Goldie's is a pretty small space. She must be using an expansion spell for the night, I thought as I watched Chester the deaf Centaur and H'rux the Minotaur walk through the door and somehow find space at one of the tall standing tables.

Goldie had paid for extra help and it was a good thing she had—business was booming. The Brownies she'd hired were running to and fro, serving up her special cheeseburgers and onion burgers as well as lots of frosty milkshakes in all flavors—strawberry, chocolate, vanilla and fresh cut grass which actually isn't half bad. I also saw quite a lot of crispy hay salads going out to the herbivorous Creatures in the room.

Once the eating finished, some room was cleared and the dancing started. Goldie's is set up like a 50's diner with tiny little juke boxes on every table where you can pay to pick a song. People started feeding silver pieces into the tiny machines and soon song after song was rolling out.

As the night started winding down, I found myself in the corner with Goldie herself, the two of us watching as people slow danced to *Earth Angel*, a golden oldie classic even I wasn't old enough to remember. The music was sweet and caused a sense of longing in my heart as I watched Sarah and Rath drift by, wrapped in each other's arms.

"Warms your heart to see, doesn't it?" Goldie murmured as we watched them dance. Like me she was somewhere around middle age with a full, hourglass figure and blonde hair that looked good on her although it obviously wasn't her natural color.

"Yes, it does," I said and sighed deeply.

"You know when she first came in here, she couldn't say a word? To me, anyway. Rath had to do all the talking," Goldie remarked, nodding at Sarah.

"I heard about that," I said. Sarah had confided to me that she used to have Selective Mutism—a condition that was caused by a binding spell which had kept her magic and her voice wrapped up tight. It had to do with a curse on her family which she had managed to break, with Rath's help. Now she could talk to anyone, though she still got a little shy at times.

"They make the cutest couple," Goldie said and sighed. "And me still single."

"I was thinking the same thing," I confessed. "I always thought there was time to find someone later but it looks like later is here and I have no one."

"You think you've got it bad—look at me," Goldie groused. "With a name like mine, you'd think I could have my pick but here I am without a single bear in sight—let alone three of them!" We both laughed together and she gave my shoulder a squeeze. "Don't give up, sweetie. It ain't over 'till it's over."

"Yeah, well…" I shrugged. "I'd like to believe that but practically the whole town is here tonight and I don't see anyone I'd want to date."

"What about H'rux?" she asked, nodding at the Minotaur who was standing across the room, bellowing in Chester the deaf Centaur's ear— it was really the only way to have a conversation with the elderly Creature.

"He's okay, I guess," I said, shrugging. "But he doesn't like sweets or pastries which is kind of my whole life. Plus, I'm a *little* freaked out about the idea of kissing a guy with a bull's head."

"Ah, you'd get over that soon enough—I hear he's hung like a bull, too," Goldie said, elbowing me in the ribs.

I hid a snort of laughter behind my hand.

"Goldie! You're so *bad!*"

"Not bad—just horny, sweetie," she said frankly. "Did you know that women our age sometimes get a second burst of hormones that make them hot to trot? I mean that literally—I might even be interested in a centaur. Not Chester but maybe his nephew Nathan— he's on the Town Council, you know," she added, nodding at a handsome Centaur who had dappled gray flanks and a thick chestnut beard that reached far down his muscular chest.

"Uh, I'm not sure how you could make that work," I said doubtfully. "I mean, anatomically, you know?"

"Oh, you can make it work," Goldie said with confidence. "There's a certain kind of sex sling you can use—of course, you need an enlargement spell too, in order to accommodate something that big."

"Oh my God—Goldie!" I slapped her arm and felt myself turning red as I giggled helplessly.

"I'm serious, girl—you can't go in there unprepared," she said, laughing along with me. "And of course you need a good birth control spell too. If you get preggers with a centaur baby, it's *over.*"

We spent some more time eyeing the other eligible bachelors in town: Jackson the Kraken, whose tentacles were mostly hidden since he was in his human form that night, Dave the werewolf who had to leave early before the full moon came out, Christopher, who was a Dragon and immensely wealthy in the Mortal Realm. He was handsome in a gleaming, scaly way—he was also in human form but the scales couldn't be hidden. Unfortunately, Goldie told me all he cared about was money and making more of it.

"Cold hearted," she said, shaking her head. "Nothing but hoarding more gold on his mind. It's a shame because he's really good looking if you don't mind the scales."

There were various other men and Creatures too, but none of them was appealing and many of them had already found their Heartmates—which made them permanently off limits. Once you find your Heartmate, you're tied to them for life. It's one of the magical parts of living in Hidden Hollow that I wished I could experience for myself.

"Hey, let's change the subject—this is getting me down," Goldie said after a while. "Let's talk business for a minute—are the pears ripe yet? I have customers asking me all the time when I'm going to get your special tarts in."

She was talking about a special kind of pastry I only made once a year—mainly because the pears that went into it were only ripe for one day. They grew on a magical tree I had discovered on one of my early morning walks when I had first moved to Hidden Hollow.

"I'm checking them every day," I promised her. "In fact, I'm going to check again tomorrow morning."

"You do that." Goldie nodded. "You don't want to miss them. Folks around here look forward to those tarts something fierce. They'll be damn disappointed if they don't get them."

"Don't worry—they're coming," I promised.

If you think we were being too serious about a simple fruit pastry, let me try to explain. The pears in question were a special variety that can't be grown commercially—they only sprout in the wild on magical lands like the ones around Hidden Hollow.

They're called "Golden-Skinned Warblers" because when they're ripe they have a golden, satiny skin that glows with magic and they give out a warbling, trilling note when they're picked. If they don't sing, they're not ripe and they taste as bitter and chalky as chewing on an aspirin tablet.

But when they *are* ripe, then you're in for a truly exquisite culinary experience. They're sweet as candy and they melt in your mouth. They taste delicious any way you bake or cook them and their flavor lingers on your tongue for hours after you eat even a tiny slice of one.

The only magical side-effect of the pears is that they make you sing every word you try to say after you eat them. Mostly it only lasts for an hour but the more you eat, the longer the effects linger. People can tell if someone gets more than his fair share of the Golden-Skinned Warbler tarts by how long they're sing-speaking afterwards.

I had been keeping a close eye on the tree—I was the only one who knew its location—and I was estimating that the pears would be ripe and ready to pick any day now. Once they were, I would pile as many as I could into my largest basket and take them back to the bakery to begin work. I would close up shop and spend most of the day making the special tarts with a big sign on the window letting folks know what to expect.

I wouldn't open the doors to The Lost Lamb until I had plenty of tarts ready to sell. Word usually spread like wildfire and I would have a line out the door and round the block for hours afterwards.

Tart Day, as everyone had started calling it, was extremely busy. I was glad I would have Sarah to help me this time. Last year I had been run off my feet for twelve hours straight. It was great for business but extremely bad for my back and knees.

"You just be sure you put at least two or three dozen aside for me," Goldie said to me now. "I'll keep them back for the folks who didn't get any because they were out of town on Tart Day."

"I'll do that," I promised her.

"Good. I can't wait—the whole town smells delicious when you start baking those." Goldie smiled at me. "Don't tell your Great Aunt I said it, but you're a better baker than she ever was. I can *taste* the love you put into your food."

"Well, thank you." I was touched. Goldie was kind of a Kitchen Witch herself—though she definitely had some other powers I wasn't quite sure about—so hearing her professional opinion of my baking was special to me.

Not long after that, the party broke up. I said goodbye to everyone and hugged a lot of people—I got asked about the special tarts several more times and promised they would be coming soon.

Then I left, having completely forgotten to ask anyone about the portrait or how to remove it from my bedroom wall.

CHAPTER FOUR

I walked home through the twilight, which always feels magical in Hidden Hollow. The air was cool and crisp with the scent of dried leaves, campfires, apple cider, and just a hint of snow. The bright fall leaves, their colors muted by the dusk, rustled on the trees and piled in drifts along the path I was walking on. They crunched under my feet as the chilly breeze ruffled my hair and made the tip of my nose go numb. Behind me, the lights of the town glowed golden and warm—the promise of comfort and a cozy fire burning in every hearth.

I inhaled deeply, taking the scents of Fall into my lungs. This was why I loved living in Hidden Hollow—that and the sense of community I felt and the safety and warmth of being somewhere I belonged with people I cared about and who cared about me. I told myself again that I didn't need a Heartmate—I was perfectly happy just as I was.

And I almost believed it.

It was only a ten-minute walk from Goldie's Diner to my house—I was inside and building up the magical fire which burned almost all year round in my main fireplace before I knew it.

Since I had taken a shower before I went to the party, I decided just to get into my nightgown and get some sleep. I wanted to get up early the next morning—I mean even earlier than usual—to check the pear tree. I decided I was going to bring my biggest basket too—you can only pick once from the Golden-Skinned Warbler tree before the pears start to wither and rot away, so I had to get as many as I could in one go.

I changed in the bathroom as usual, brushing my teeth and running a brush through my hair, before throwing my clothes in the dirty clothes hamper and sliding into a fresh silk nightgown.

I don't own many fancy outfits—I practically live in my cooking whites—but I like to splurge on my underwear. The gown was pure white silk that fell to my knees. It had spaghetti straps and a plunging V neckline that showed the creamy inner curves of my large breasts.

Despite hitting forty, I was still fairly perky up top—probably thanks to the magical herbs that Madam Healer supplied me with. The dark points of my nipples could be seen tenting the pale gown and the silk felt especially good against my sensitive peaks tonight.

Maybe Goldie is right, I thought as I cupped my breasts and thumbed the tight points lightly, sending a shiver of desire down my spine. *Maybe women our age **do** get extra horny.*

I certainly felt it tonight. My nipples tingled with desire and between my legs I felt hot and wet and ready. I moaned softly as I plucked lightly at my tight tips. I might not have a Heartmate to help me out, but I knew how to please myself. I kept a toy collection that would be the envy of any porn star in the drawer of my nightstand. Tonight I was going to use every toy, I told myself. I wanted to draw out the pleasure and make it last…

At least, that was my intention until I stepped into my bedroom and was confronted with the portrait of the Demon hanging on my wall.

"Well, Hell!" I snapped at it, when I saw his handsome face looking down at me with a mocking smile. "I forgot all about you!"

Well, I would just ignore the picture, I told myself as I built up the fire in my bedroom fireplace. It was only a portrait after all—it wasn't like the Demon was actually *watching* me.

Only he *seemed* to be. I could have sworn his blazing black eyes were following me with every move I made. He seemed to be staring down at me from his place on the wall, watching as I slid into the bed and reached for my toy drawer.

I was determined not to care, though—he was just a *picture* and I was really horny. I was *not* going to get shy and embarrassed because of a stupid painting!

I picked out one of my favorite starting toys—a small but strong vibe that strapped to my index finger. I liked to use it to tease my nipples and clit, edging myself for a while before I moved on to something larger and more powerful.

But this time as I rubbed the buzzing tip of the little finger vibe around my aching peaks, I felt like the Demon was watching me. The look in his painted eyes was almost *hungry* as I lay on the bed across from him and teased myself.

No, stop it, I scolded myself mentally. *He's not watching—you're being crazy. Ignore him and concentrate.*

But it was hard to take my own advice. I was lying on top of the patchwork quilt that covered my bed with my legs spread and the top of my nightgown pulled down to bare my breasts as I touched myself, but I found that I couldn't concentrate on any of my usual fantasies.

Giving up on my regular erotic daydreams, I tried imagining what it would be like with H'rux the Minotaur—on my hands and knees with that big, bull's head hanging over my shoulder, as he pumped his bull-sized cock into my willing pussy and his heavy balls slapped against my swollen clit. And then I thought about Jackson the Kraken —what would it feel like to have all those tentacles teasing me at once? Sucking at my nipples and sliding between my legs to tease my aching button...

I even tried picturing sex with a Centaur using the special sex sling that Goldie had talked about. I wondered if it strapped you in position beneath the centaur in question with your legs spread wide as you watched that enormous cock plowing into you...

But somehow nothing was working. Why couldn't I concentrate on a fantasy to get me over the edge tonight?

"It's *your* fault," I told the painted Demon, looking down on my bed. "You're the reason I can't get off!"

Spreading my legs, I reached for another, much larger vibe. This one stretched me to the limit and I gave a muffled moan as I fit the bulbous head to the mouth of my pussy and pushed inward. This time, instead of trying to picture myself with any of the men I knew or usually fantasized about, I looked at the picture of the handsome Demon instead.

I imagined him on the bed with me—spreading my thighs to taste me while I gripped his horns and begged for more. Maybe he would tease me with that tail of his—what exactly did it do? Was the pointed end hard or soft—did it poke or caress... or both?

This time I found it much easier to reach the edge...but I still couldn't tip over into the pleasure that was calling to me. I tried and tried, thrusting the thick vibe deeper into my pussy as the little rabbit ears attached to the middle of it buzzed my aching clit. But no matter what I did, my orgasm eluded me.

Frustrated at last, I pulled the toy out of me and put it back in the drawer. Tomorrow I would take time to clean everything thoroughly but tonight I needed to get to sleep. If I didn't, I was going to be dead on my feet at work.

Giving the Demon a last dirty look, I slid under the quilt and rolled over on my side. My sexual frustration kept me awake for a while but then it started to rain outside and the steady sound of the falling drops and the distant rumble of thunder at last relaxed me.

I was just drifting off to sleep when an enormous bolt of lightning struck right outside my bedroom window followed by the *crack* and *boom* of thunder. It shook the house violently and I gasped and sat bolt upright in bed—just as the heavy portrait fell off the wall and landed on the hardwood of the bedroom with a *thud!*

"Oh my God!" I gasped, jumping out of bed. The portrait had fallen forward and was flat on the floor. Struggling mightily, I managed to heave it upright again so that it was balanced on its bottom edge.

I examined the front of it. In the light from my bedroom fire, I could see a long, jagged crack running diagonally across the face of the Demon.

"Well, damn," I muttered to myself. "So much for not damaging the family heirloom."

I reached up to touch the crack, trying to see how bad it was, and felt a sharp pain in my index finger.

"Ouch!" I gasped, pulling back to shove my hurt finger into my mouth. The last thing I needed was a cut finger when I had to be baking and kneading dough tomorrow!

I sucked my finger resentfully as I studied the smudge of blood I had left on the Demon's smug face.

"Yeah, very funny," I told him, after taking my finger out of my mouth and examining it. "That's a nice way to thank me for picking you up off the floor!"

Then I realized I was talking to a picture—probably because I was still half asleep. I decided then and there I was going to lean the portrait against the wall with the back of it to me and the Demon facing the wall. That way I didn't have to see his irritatingly handsome face while I drifted back to sleep.

It took all my strength—and I'm not weak, I regularly work with fifty-pound sacks of flour and huge balls of dough—but I finally got the picture turned around and leaned against the wall.

I was just about to go back to bed, when an inscription on the back of the picture caught my eye. I frowned and squinted, leaning forward to see that someone had written a verse on the back in faded black ink.

The handwriting was thin and spidery and I shouldn't have been able to read it in the light of my dying fire. But as I looked at the words, they seemed to almost glow in the dark and I found myself reading the verse aloud.

"Hester's blood shall call me forth,
Break me from my prison glass.
Turn my portrait towards the North,
Let my Lust consume the lass.
By her side, will I stay
And her fantasy fulfill
I will not leave until the day
She has had her lustful will."

"Well, that's weird," I muttered to myself as I stood and brushed myself off. I had a sudden thought—had I turned the picture towards the North? Unfortunately I have a negative sense of direction, meaning I can get lost at the drop of a hat. I had no idea what direction North was, but I wasn't worried about it. It was just another weird thing about the strange portrait my Great Aunt had left me.

Well, at least it was no longer glued to my wall.

"Tomorrow you're going straight up in the attic," I told the portrait. "You've cost me enough sleep as it is!"

Still grumbling to myself and sucking my hurt finger I crawled back into bed. I drifted off to sleep again...only to have the most erotic dream of my life.

CHAPTER FIVE

S omeone was touching me—not just touching me, *holding* me, just
the way I longed to be held. A big, warm body was curled around
my own, spooning me. I could feel the hard wall of a muscular chest
against my back and a big hand was reaching around to cup one of my
breasts through the thin silk of my nightgown.

"*Mmm*, you feel so good in my arms, baby," a deep, growling voice
rumbled in my ear. "Been wanting to hold you for so damn long…"

It was another one of the erotic dreams that had been plaguing me
for the past six months, I realized sleepily. Only this time I seemed to
be actually experiencing it as an active participant—not just an
observer. Which was nice—*really* nice.

I had gone to sleep still horny due to my inability to reach a release
and now I felt my need rushing over me again. The man behind me
smelled so good—like a campfire in the woods at night and some
warm, dark spice that was completely masculine. His scent seemed to
trigger something inside me—a deeper lust than anything I had ever
felt before. Suddenly I was nearly panting with desire.

Arching my back, I rubbed against him, pressing my ass to the hard lump I could feel growing behind me. God, he felt *huge.* Even bigger than the Creatures I'd been imagining as I touched myself earlier.

"I can be as big as you want me to be, baby," he growled softly and I realized he was somehow reading my mind. "Is that what you need? A nice thick cock filling your tight little pussy? Is that your fantasy?"

I absolutely *love* it when a man talks dirty to me—this dream was getting more realistic and better all the time, I thought as I rubbed against him.

"Yes," I moaned softly. "That's what I need!"

"*Mmm*, but we need to get you all warmed up first, sweetheart." His second hand slipped around my hip and he turned me so that I was on my back and looking up at him. His handsome face in the flickering light of the dying fire looked strangely familiar, but there were too many shadows to be for sure.

"Look at you, all spread out for me," he murmured, smoothing one big, warm hand down my body. I could feel his heat through the thin silk of my gown—his touch raised chill bumps on my skin as he slowly caressed my breasts, plucking lightly at the nipples to make me moan and squirm. "Spread those gorgeous thick thighs for me," he ordered softly. "Let me feel that soft little pussy I've been dreaming about."

Helpless to disobey, I spread my legs for him. He skimmed one big hand down my belly and then long fingers were sliding between my thighs to cup my mound through my nightgown.

"Hmm, now what have we here? Are you wet for me, baby?" he rumbled and I felt him parting my pussy lips with surprising delicacy, considering how big his hand was.

I moaned softly as he stroked my aching clit through the thin silk of my gown. Why wouldn't he reach under it to stroke my bare pussy? I shifted my hips and writhed under his gentle, teasing touch.

Somehow he seemed to understand what I wanted because I heard a deep rumble of laughter.

"Eager little thing, aren't you?" he murmured, stroking me deeper but still keeping the silk gown between us. "Damn, your soft little pussy is so wet for me! And you're being such a good girl, spreading so wide to let me pet you."

"Please!" I whispered, writhing under his touch. "I...I don't know who you are but this feels so good. Why can't you touch me without the gown in the way?"

"Oh, you want me to pet your sweet pussy with nothing between us? I think that can be arranged," he rumbled. "But first I want to suck those tight nipples.

He bent his head over me and I thought there was something strange about it. Was he wearing some kind of hat? What were those things coming out either side of his forehead?

But the next minute I was arching my back and panting as he sucked one ripe tip into his mouth and began circling my nipple with his tongue. His mouth felt hotter than I would have expected—almost as though he was on fire with lust inside. Then he moved to my other peak, teasing and nipping it very lightly before sucking hard to take as much of my breast as he could into his hot mouth.

At the same time he was sucking my nipples, his hand was still moving, lightly tracing my aching clit through my gown. Then, finally, the hand moved away and I was sure I knew what was coming next.

I expected my dream lover to pull up my gown with his hand to touch my bare pussy, but instead, something else—another appendage —came sliding around my hip to lift the soaked silk away from the apex of my thighs.

I squinted in the dimness, trying to make out what was lifting my gown. It wasn't a hand...what *was* it?

At that moment, a log in the fireplace broke, sending up a shower of sparks and brightening the room. Suddenly I could see more clearly. The appendage lifting my gown was long and whip-like. It also had a triangular pointed end and it moved with the sinuous grace of a snake.

Oh my God, I thought blankly. *A tail—that's a tail. He's got a **tail!***

And just as I thought it, the tip of the tail whipped down and stung me—right on my clit!

My shriek of surprise turned immediately into a moan of intense pleasure. The sting my dream lover had given me had resulted in an inner explosion—an orgasm stronger and sharper than anything I had ever felt in my life.

It cracked through me like a lightning bolt, electrifying my whole body and making my back arch and my toes curl helplessly. It felt like every muscle in my body was spasming at once as the pleasure shot through me. At one point it felt like even my *hair* was coming and I started to see black spots dancing before my eyes.

And that was when I knew I wasn't dreaming anymore. Nobody experiences Category Five orgasms in their sleep. Or nobody I'd ever heard of before, anyway.

"This…is not…not a dream," I panted, struggling to get my breath back.

"No, of course not." In the light from the fire, I saw the face of the Demon in the painting smiling down at me smugly. "This is your fantasy, Celia, and I'm here to fulfill it."

CHAPTER SIX

"Get away from me!" I gasped, shoving at his broad chest as I scrambled away. I rolled off the edge of the bed and would have fallen if he hadn't reached out one long arm and caught me by the waist.

"Take it easy, baby—breathe!" he urged, pulling me firmly back onto the bed.

"I don't want to breathe! I want you *out* of here!" I pointed a trembling finger at the bedroom door.

But the Demon from the painting wasn't going anywhere.

"Sorry, I can't go," he drawled, not sounding sorry at all. "I'm here until I fulfill your deepest fantasy—the one you hide deep down inside, even from yourself."

"What? What are you talking about? And who *are* you?" I demanded. Which would have been good questions to ask *before* I let him suck my nipples and sting my clit with his tail.

Speaking of that, my clit was still tingling and throbbing—it was like my body was threatening to come again at any minute. Which I definitely did *not* need right now—especially since the other orgasm he'd given me had nearly made me faint with pleasure.

"I am Malik—Incubus extraordinaire at your service." He bowed from the waist, the firelight gleaming on his curving horns and the broad, bare planes of his muscular chest. I realized suddenly he was naked.

"Hey—where are your clothes? Where's your suit with the lacy cravat?" I said, making a gesture at my own throat to indicate the frothy lace.

"I took it off, of course." He shrugged, his broad shoulders rolling. "I thought it would be easier to fulfill your fantasy without it on."

"Well put it back on!" I snapped. "You're not fulfilling anything tonight."

He sighed.

"And here I thought this assignment would be easy. You looked so eager—so *hungry*—lying there on the bed earlier with your thighs spread, teasing your soft little pussy just for me."

"I was not doing...what I was doing for *you*," I said stiffly. "I thought you were just a picture—just paint on canvas. I didn't know you were actually *watching me!*"

"Come on, how could you not know?" he asked, sounding entirely too reasonable. "You woke me with your touch. Didn't you feel the tingle of magic when you did it? Didn't you see my eyes following you?"

"No, I didn't," I said, lying through my teeth—about the tingling, at least.

In retrospect, I could see that I should have been more concerned about it. But after living in Hidden Hollow for five years, I had more or less gotten used to magic being performed around me all the time. So feeling a tingle when I touched his portrait hadn't worried me.

I was feeling really stupid about that right now.

"Look," I said, glaring at him. "I'm sorry if I woke you up somehow —that certainly wasn't my intention. But I'm going to have to ask you to leave now. I have no interest in having you fulfill any of my, er, fantasies or anything else. So please just go."

"Sorry, I can't. I'm tied to your bloodline." He shrugged again—a "what can you do?" gesture that made me clench my jaw in irritation.

"What do you mean you're tied to my bloodline?" I demanded. "Are you saying I inherited you somehow? Inherited a *Demon?*"

"An *Incubus*," he corrected me. "And yes, that's exactly what you did —you inherited me."

"I'm sure my Great Aunt Gertrude never meant for me to have *you*," I protested. "She just left me your picture—she didn't know a real-life Demon lived inside it!"

"*Incubus*. And I think she had her suspicions." He sounded thoughtful. "I know she was careful never to waken me fully or to set me free. I think she got so thoroughly sick of males during her disastrous marriage that she never wanted one in her life again."

I had to admit, that *did* sound like Great Aunt Gertrude. But then, why had she saddled *me* with the Demonic portrait and its annoying inhabitant?

Annoying but hot, whispered a traitorous little voice in my head as I watched him from the corner of my eye. I couldn't help admiring the way the firelight shone on the golden-red skin of the Demon's muscular body. And if that shadow I saw between his legs was any indication, he really might give a Centaur or a Minotaur some serious competition in the size department.

But my perusal hadn't gone unnoticed.

"Admit it—you like what you see. You *want* me to fulfill your deepest fantasy—*that's* why your Great Aunt left me to you," he rumbled, giving me a half-lidded look that seemed to promise all kinds of erotic acts no other man had ever offered me.

"Are you reading my mind?" I demanded, glaring at him.

"I don't have to read your mind—your thoughts are clearly written on your lovely face," he murmured.

Which wasn't exactly an answer.

"Look, I don't care why Great Aunt Gertrude left you to me, the fact is I don't *want* you here," I said impatiently.

"That's too bad—I can't leave until I fulfill the terms of the wish your many times great grandmother, Hester Hatch, made centuries ago," he said firmly. "I am tied to the women of your bloodline—I cannot be free until I give you what you so desperately need."

"I'm not *desperate* for anyone!" I snapped, offended. "Least of all some gigolo Demon who's been spying on me from a painting!"

"Please, I'm an *Incubus,*" he corrected me again.

I threw up my hands in frustration.

"Demon, Incubus—what's the difference?"

"The difference is, I am several steps above a lowly Demon," he said, sounding slightly offended. "I am a *specialist*. Only a witch with considerable power can summon me."

"I'm just a Kitchen Witch," I pointed out. "I make pastries and run a bakery—that's pretty much it."

"You may be 'just a Kitchen Witch' but you have the whole town in your thrall," he said, smiling. "They all come flocking to your bakery for your delicious pastries just as they flocked to your birthday party tonight."

"How do you know that?" I narrowed my eyes at him suspiciously. "You shouldn't know any of that if I just woke you up a little while ago."

"I learned it when I was pleasuring you." His eyes went half-lidded again. "You're so sensitive—you reacted beautifully to my touch."

I could feel my cheeks getting hot with mortification.

"I thought I was having a dream," I said stiffly. "So are you saying you *can* read my mind?" I asked, trying to change the subject.

"Only when I'm touching you," he admitted. "Mind reading is one of an Incubus's most valuable skills."

"What? Why is that?" I asked, curious despite myself.

He shrugged.

"Isn't it obvious? A mortal male doesn't know what you want in bed unless you spell it out for him—and even then he's more than likely to get it wrong. Whereas when *I* touch you, I can tell what you're hungry for—what you *crave.*"

"You…you can?" I asked through numb lips. God, I wished he wasn't so mouthwatering sitting there nude and muscular in my bed!

"Mmm-hmm." He nodded and leaned towards me, the firelight reflected in his black eyes. "And I can give it to you, baby—whether it's a hard fuck or a long, leisurely lovemaking session where you come over and over and cry in my arms from the intense release afterwards," he murmured, giving me another one of those lustful looks. "Or maybe you just want your pussy licked for hours on end—I can do that for you too." His eyes blazed. "I *love* it—love to worship the female body with all its lovely curves. Especially fuller curves like yours." He described an overfull hourglass in the air between us as he looked me up and down.

I pulled the top of my nightgown closed and leaned away from him but my heart was pounding. He had just given me the most intense orgasm of my life and yet here I was, hot to trot—as Goldie would say —all over again!

"Don't talk like that—I don't even *know* you," I protested.

"But *I* know *you*, Celia. I know what you're craving—why don't you let me give it to you?" he murmured.

"Because I don't have sex with strangers!" I snapped. "And besides, I'm *not* craving anything like…like that."

"Please. Don't lie to me or yourself." He shook his head. "Your lust perfumes the air between us and I saw the way you touched yourself earlier—saw the way you *fucked* yourself with that toy of yours."

His voice was a low, sexy rasp and his eyes were blazing again—challenging me to deny what he was saying.

I was torn between mortification and lust, which was creeping up on me even though I didn't want to feel it.

"You weren't *supposed* to see that," I said. "I didn't know you were watching!"

"You can tell yourself that, but you know it's not true. And until you give in and let me fulfill your fantasy we won't be free of each other," he pointed out. "So why not lay back and let me worship your body in the way you deserve? I bet no other male has ever truly given you your due."

As a matter of fact, he was right about that. I'd never had a lover who was really eager to go down on me or give me pleasure. Maybe because trying to find the right guy when you're plus-sized is like dating on hard mode. I'd met plenty of men who would have been happy just to use my body for their own gratification...but none that were very interested in mine.

But this Demon—this Incubus—was telling me that he was all about my gratification—all about giving me pleasure in any way I wanted it. Malik didn't seem to mind that I was curvy—in fact he seemed to *like* it.

I couldn't help remembering how good it felt when he touched me...the hot swirl of his tongue around my sensitive nipples and the expert way he'd stroked my pussy, circling my clit in a way that drove me crazy, touching me just the right way...

No, what was I thinking? He was getting to me—I couldn't let that happen!

"Absolutely not," I said firmly. "In fact, I want you to get dressed and leave *right now.*"

He sighed.

"So you're going to make this difficult for both of us? All right. I can get dressed but I can't leave—not until I fulfill your fantasy and Hester's wish."

"What did she wish for, anyway?" I demanded. I had never given much thought to my ancestress. All I knew was that she was a Kitchen Witch like me and that she'd been hung during the Witch Fever that had swept New England back in the 1600s.

"I can show you, if you like," he offered. "Maybe if you see her and what happened to her you'll finally understand why I'm bound to your family."

"How can you show me?" I asked suspiciously. "Do you have to transport me back in time or something?" I wasn't eager to travel to the 1600s—especially not dressed in my sheer silk nightgown. I'd been to several museums in Salem that convinced me life was dirty, dark, and dismal back then. Also, they treated women like dirt. No thank you!

But Malik only laughed.

"Hardly. My powers don't extend quite that far. I can't take you back in time but I can *show* you what I saw…and what happened to Hester, your ancestress."

"Well…" I hesitated but it didn't seem like I was getting rid of him any time soon. Maybe if I had more information, I'd have a better chance of banishing him from my life. "All right," I said at last. "How do you do it?"

"Just hold my hand and I'll show you." He held out a large, well-shaped hand but I pulled back.

"First put on some clothes," I told him. I had a strange feeling that if I touched him, the lust I was feeling would overcome me and I might try to jump his demonic bones. I needed some barriers between us so that couldn't happen.

He sighed again.

"Very well. But not the suit I wore in the painting—it's horribly uncomfortable and I was wearing it for *centuries*."

"I thought you were asleep," I said suspiciously.

"I was dozing," he said. "I didn't fully awaken until you touched me. And gave me your blood and turned my portrait towards the North, fulfilling the first part of the spell and allowing me to leave my prison of glass."

"But I never…" I trailed off, remembering how I had cut my finger on the broken glass and left a smear of blood on the portrait. And apparently turning his picture towards the wall had been turning it towards the North. Damn it, I needed to invest in a compass or at least be more careful around strange magic!

"Here—what about this?" He snapped his fingers and suddenly he was wearing a different kind of suit. It was an expensive tailored one that wouldn't have looked out of place on a billionaire on the cover of a romance novel. It was black with a crisp white Egyptian cotton shirt and a maroon tie. Diamond cufflinks glinted at his wrists and the scent of expensive cologne, mixed with his aroma of smoke and spice, filled my senses.

What is it about a man in a suit? My mind was suddenly filled with fantasies of calling him "Sir" and having him bend me over his knee to "punish" me with a spanking because I had been a "bad girl."

I shook my head, trying to drive the illicit images away. I just hoped he couldn't read my mind when we weren't touching. But I couldn't stop staring at him.

"*Wow,*" I murmured, rendered temporarily speechless—or at least monosyllabic.

"Thank you." He flashed me a gleaming grin. "That's a most gratifying reaction. Now, will you allow me to show you the fate of your ancestress all those many years ago?"

He held out his hand again and this time, reluctantly, I took it.

"Good—thank you for trusting me." Malik smiled and entwined our fingers, his much larger hand swallowing my own. "Now hold on tight—you might get dizzy."

"Dizzy? Why?" I asked.

But before the words fully left my mouth, the room started spinning around me in a colorful, kaleidoscope swirl and then the world around me disappeared...

CHAPTER SEVEN

"Oh my God!" I gasped. Malik was right—I was intensely dizzy!

"It's all right—I've got you." Strong arms wrapped around me and suddenly he was pulling me into his lap.

I wanted to fight and struggle but the world was still spinning and I was afraid if he let go of me I'd go flying off into the black void that had suddenly appeared around us. So instead of flinging myself away from him, I shrank back against his big body.

He really was huge—even bigger than I'd imagined when I looked at his portrait, I thought distractedly. Being a curvy girl, it takes a lot to make me feel petite but Malik managed it. He held me securely in his lap making me feel safe even though I still didn't know him very well.

At last the swirling stopped and I found myself in the middle of a kitchen. At least, I *thought* it was a kitchen. There was no refrigerator or sink or any other modern appliances like a microwave or a dishwasher. There was, however, a large fireplace—a "hearth" to use the old-fashioned word, which was the only one that seemed to fit. A low fire was burning in the grate and some kind of animal—maybe a rabbit—was spitted over it.

There was a rough wooden table in the middle of the room that looked handmade and straw scattered over the hard packed dirt floor. A woman wearing a plain gray dress with a white collar and a white cap was leaning over the table, chopping some kind of squash with a crude metal knife. She was humming softly to herself and though I couldn't see her face because of the cap, I knew at once that this was Hester, my many times great grandmother.

"There she is," Malik murmured in my ear. "Poor little Hester. She had a dreary life, I fear. But then, so did all Puritan women. They were owned by their husbands, you know and unfortunately many of the men didn't treat their wives very well."

As if the Demon's words had called to him, the door of the wooden house banged open and a tall man in a plain black suit and a wide white collar came in. He was wearing one of those tall hats with a buckle on it that you always see on people playing Pilgrims at Thanksgiving but he took it off when he came in the house.

"Hester!" he snapped, frowning at the woman at the table. "Why is my dinner not ready? A man works hard all day—the least he can expect is to have dinner to warm his belly when the long day is finally done!"

"Forgive me, John!" Hester looked up and now I could see that she had eyes the same color of blue as my own. There was a frightened, resentful look on her face but she didn't drop her eyes when her husband scowled at her. "The rabbit is nearly done and the corn pudding is finished too," she went on. "I was just going to add a bit of squash and butter to a pot—"

"Forget the squash—I'm hungry *now*," he snarled. "Hurry up and serve me, woman!"

Grabbing a rickety looking wooden chair from against the wall, he sat down at the table and looked up at her expectantly.

Hester looked like she wanted to say something but didn't quite dare. Instead she went about serving him silently. She sliced some meat off the roasting rabbit and scooped what I assumed must be the corn pudding—it looked like mush—onto the pewter plate beside it.

Despite its simplicity, the food smelled delicious—not surprising considering that Hester was a Kitchen Witch, I thought.

She put the plate down in front of him but her husband wasn't satisfied.

"Where's my ale, woman?" he demanded, glaring at her. "Are thee hoping I will choke to death with nothing to wash my dinner down?"

"No, of course not, John. But I thought maybe thou might prefer water?"

"Why would I want water when there's ale to quench my thirst? Get me some now!" he demanded.

"She was hoping he wouldn't get drunk and beat her," Malik murmured in my ear, answering my unasked question. "That was legal in those times, you know."

"It still happens now," I pointed out. "But I can see how difficult it would be if you couldn't even go to the police. Er, did he beat her a lot?"

"Not too often but when he did it was severe," Malik murmured. "Mostly he just ignored her until he wanted something. He wasn't a very pleasant man to live with, I'm afraid."

We watched as Hester poured a mug of ale for her husband—who I supposed must be my many times great grandfather, though I felt no connection to him at all. With Hester it was different. I felt *akin* to her —I guess was the best way to put it. It was like there was a golden thread tying us together—maybe it was the blood connection we shared, even though she had lived so many hundreds of years before me.

At that point several girls and a boy came in, also clambering for food. They shut up when they saw their father though—clearly they knew better than to disturb John Hatch.

Hester fed them all and ate a little herself. Nobody talked except when John demanded more ale and another slice of rabbit. The only noise was the scraping of the crude metal silverware against the pewter plates.

"As you can see, it wasn't a very happy home," Malik murmured in my ear. "I think this might be part of what started Hester wishing for more than her husband was willing to give her. Here—you'll see what I mean."

The world swirled around us and the scene changed. Now we were in a bedroom with one of the old-fashioned beds like the kind I'd seen in the museum in Salem. They had ropes instead of a box spring and you tightened them at night to make the straw or feather stuffed mattress firmer. (If you're interested, this was where the saying "sleep tight" comes from—or anyway, that's what the museum guide told me.)

Hester was wearing a long white gown and a white nightcap. She was already in bed when her husband came into the room wearing a long nightshirt that showed his pale, hairy legs. It was dark outside and the only light was from the fireplace on the far side of the room.

John got into bed beside Hester and turned to her.

"Spread thy legs, woman. I would take my husbandly due."

He gestured at her abruptly and I saw Hester's face go red. But she did as she was told, spreading her legs and raising her nightgown above her hips. Without any kind of foreplay, her husband climbed on top of her and began thrusting.

Hester didn't say a word but the look on her face nearly broke my heart—it was an expression of pain and longing, as though she was imagining something better—something more and yet knew she was never going to get it.

"The bastard!" Malik's voice was surprisingly angry in my ear.

I turned to look at him and saw that his handsome face was twisted into a mask of rage and disgust.

"Look at him—he didn't even *try* to get her ready," he growled, nodding at the couple on the bed. I could hear the ropes that served as the base of it creaking as John continued thrusting vigorously. "No *wonder* she longed for me—called for me, even though she didn't know she was calling," Malik went on. "She wished for more than this—she wished for love and pleasure and a man who cared enough to give her both. But she never got it."

"Then…you *didn't* have sex with her?" I asked hesitantly.

He shook his head.

"I wouldn't be here now if I'd been able to fulfill her longings. As I said, she called for me before she died, but I didn't arrive in time to save her—or to fulfill her fantasy."

"What happened then?" I asked. "I mean, why was she hanged?"

"Ah, well that would be because of the gooseberry pie incident," he murmured mysteriously.

"What? What gooseberry pie incident?" I asked, frowning.

"It was a pie she baked for a church get together," he explained. "She must have been having lustful thoughts when she baked it because when they served it…well, I'll let you see."

He held me tight and the world swirled again to reveal a scene that reminded me a little of the depictions you always see of the "First Thanksgiving." People in dark, sober clothing were seated on benches on either side of a long wooden table. There were platters of food in the center of the table and a man standing at the end was giving a rather long-winded prayer of thanks as everyone else kept their heads bowed and their eyes shut.

"And we thank thee for thy bounty. Please bless it to our bodies that we may be strengthened and continue to do thy work in this world," the minister, (at least I assumed it was the minister—he had the biggest hat and the sternest face,) finished at last. He sat down and everyone dug in.

As they ate, I couldn't help noticing a large juicy looking pie with a flaky brown latticework crust at the far end of the table near Hester. John was sitting beside her and the minister who had said grace wasn't far from them.

"Is this thy pie, Goody Hatch?" an elderly woman beside Hester asked, reaching for a slice of it.

"Indeed it is, Goody Ward. The gooseberries were bountiful this year." Hester nodded politely. "I hope thee enjoys it."

"Unfortunately, they did *more* than enjoy it," Malik murmured in my ear. "Keep and eye on Goody Ward there—she was a matriarch of the village with a reputation considered beyond reproach. Well, until *this* happened."

I watched as the woman—who looked older than anyone else at the table—took a big bite of the pie.

At first there was no effect but then she murmured, "Oh, my!" and began tugging at the modest white collar around her neck.

Other people got slices of the pie as well—though the minister refused a slice when Hester offered.

"Nay, Goody Hatch," he said importantly. "I am denying myself the pleasures of the flesh so I must not eat thy pie, delicious-looking though it may be."

But a lot of other people did have slices. As they ate, they all started tugging at their clothes—loosening them as though they were getting overheated, although it felt like a cool fall day to me.

Suddenly the older lady—Goody Ward—who had been the first to eat the pie, lurched to her feet. She climbed clumsily off the bench and made a beeline for the minister who was at the head of the table.

"Goody Ward? Are thee well?" The minister looked up at her with obvious concern on his stern face.

"Ah, Reverend Smith!" she exclaimed, reaching for him. "I *long* for thee!"

"What?" He gaped at her, clearly startled.

But Goody Ward had already begun undressing. She pulled open the plain brown dress she was wearing, revealing pendulous breasts which she thrust into the minister's face.

Reverend Smith was so surprised he fell off his bench and into the dirt.

"By God, woman! What art thou doing?" he demanded, looking up at her.

But Goody Ward wasn't going to be denied. She bent over him, dangling her breasts in his shocked face.

"Thou art a man to set any woman's loins ablaze," she moaned. "Many a time have I thought so as I watched thee in the pulpit of a Sunday!"

"The Devil has possessed thee!" Reverend Smith exclaimed, looking even more shocked.

But it wasn't only Goody Ward who was affected. Other people at the table who had eaten the gooseberry pie were also getting busy. There was a whole impromptu Puritan orgy happening right there at the long wooden table. People who clearly weren't married—but who had possibly been lusting for each other—were going at it.

I saw a man lift a woman's dress and push her down over the table, smashing her face in a dish of buttered mashed pumpkin as he thrust into her from behind. On another bench, a woman had straddled a man who was clearly not her husband and was riding him right there, moaning with lust as she bucked her hips to take him deeper.

All up and down the long table, Puritans were fucking. And I mean, they were *really* going for it to the horror of the others at the table.

The people who *hadn't* eaten the gooseberry pie were clearly appalled and unsure of what was happening. But the ones that had taken even a bite, had lost all their inhibitions.

"This is what called to me," Malik said in my ear. "This outpouring of lust and longing. I felt Hester's sexual need tugging at me all the way from Hell's Waiting Room."

"Hell's Waiting Room—what's that?" I asked, frowning.

"Well the place we upper order demonic entities wait for assignments, of course," he said, as though it should be obvious. "But it takes time to get from there to the Mortal Realm. By the time I ascended from the depths, Hester had already been blamed for "The Devil's Lusty Pie" as they were calling the incident. I wanted to save her but there was a witch finder by the name of Milas James waiting for me. It was he who trapped me in the portrait for so many years. Until *you* let me out."

"I didn't do it on purpose," I muttered, suddenly aware all over again of how close we were, with me sitting in his lap.

"Nevertheless I thank you," he rumbled. "It's good to be free and awake again after so many long, weary centuries."

"You could thank me by leaving," I suggested. "By going back to 'Hell's Waiting Room.'"

"I've already explained why I can't do that. Unless you want me to fulfill your deepest fantasy now?" he asked, giving me a sinfully sexy smile.

I felt a sudden surge of lust and wondered if it was coming from him. It *must* be, damn it! There was no way I was getting horny just because I was sitting on the big Demon's lap and hearing his deep voice in my ear…

"No," I said shortly. "In fact, I want you to take me home."

"We're already in your home, but I will turn the clock back to where we started. Hold on," Malik murmured.

The world started spinning again and I gave a muffled gasp and grabbed his arms, which were wrapped securely around me.

"It's all right, baby," I heard him say. "I've got you—I won't let you go."

Which was exactly what I was afraid of.

The spinning seemed to last longer this time. When it finally stopped, I was so dizzy I could barely see straight.

"Oh!" I moaned, putting a hand to my forehead. "I feel awful!"

"I'm so sorry, Celia—I forgot how difficult it is for a mortal to see into the past and then come back to the present." Malik sounded genuinely contrite as he laid me gently on my side. "Just relax," he murmured in my ear. "Close your eyes and rest. You'll feel better soon."

I did as he said—what choice did I have when I was so dizzy I couldn't even sit up? But somehow the relaxing turned into a deep sleepiness that overtook me. I warned myself to stay awake—I needed to find a way to get rid of the pesky Incubus and I was never going to do that if I fell asleep.

But no matter how I lectured myself about staying awake, my eyelids were just too heavy. It seemed that seeing into the past had tired me out tremendously and my body just wasn't willing to fight the weariness that was dragging me down into sleep like an anchor tied around my legs.

At last, I had to give up.

Tomorrow, I told myself. *I'll get rid of him tomorrow.*

I had no idea that I would have a whole new set of problems the next day that would completely take my mind off my uninvited house guest.

CHAPTER EIGHT

I woke up bright and early thanks to my alarm. But honestly, even without the *Ding-ding-a-ding-a-ding-ding-a-ding* I still probably would have been up. I've been a baker too long to be able to sleep in. Even on the one day a week I take off, I still wake up at the crack of dawn.

Strangely, the first thing on my mind *wasn't* Malik or the adventure he'd taken me on, into the past the night before. That all seemed like a dream to me—one that was already fading from my mind.

What I was most concerned about at the moment was the Golden-Skinned Warbler Pears—I had a very strong feeling that today was the day they would be ripe. Call it whatever you want—women's intuition or a witch's instinct—either way I had learned to trust my gut and the feeling was too strong to ignore.

But still, the dream lingered—it was too strange not to. I sat on the side of the bed, rubbing sleep out of my eyes, and looked up at the wall, expecting to see the portrait hanging there and the smug-faced Demon staring down at me.

Only a blank spot on my wall greeted me. And when I let my eyes drift downward, I saw an empty picture frame with cracked glass.

I put my head in my hands and let out a groan—oh no, it *hadn't* been a dream after all! But if that was so, then where was Malik now?

A quick check revealed he wasn't in bed beside me. The quilt and sheets were rumpled, as though someone had been lying there but he was gone. Where was he then? The bathroom? Did Demons have to go, like humans did? There was only one way to find out.

A look in the bathroom showed it to be empty and the rest of the house was likewise lacking evidence of any supernaturally sexy demonic presence. I began to have a cautious sense of optimism. Maybe Malik was gone for good. He must have been lying when he claimed he had to fulfill my deepest, darkest fantasy and when he realized I wasn't going to sleep with him, he'd decided to skip town.

The thought filled me with a confusing mixture of relief and regret. After all, it had been a long time since any man had showed me such intense sexual interest. It was nice to feel so desirable—it spoke to the core of my femininity to be lusted after like that.

Then I gave myself a mental kick—what was I thinking? What I had told Malik the night before about *not* sleeping with strangers still held true. I had too much dignity for that, I told myself firmly. I was *not* going to allow myself to be sucked into a sexual relationship— however brief—with a man I didn't know. Especially since the man in question wasn't even a man—he was an Incubus—a sex Demon.

*Only you **do** know him—in a way,* whispered that contrary little voice in the back of my head. *Haven't you been dreaming about him for the past six months?*

It was true, I realized as the half-formed dreams I hadn't been able to remember suddenly came rushing back. Malik had been in every one of them, taunting me, teasing me, doing all kinds of erotic things to my body no man had ever done before…

"No!" I said out loud and then jumped at the sound of my own voice echoing through the empty house. Empty—that's right, the house was *empty* because Malik was *gone.* So it was time to stop stressing over a problem that had solved itself and go check on the pear tree.

I slapped on a little makeup and put my hair up in ponytail. Then I got dressed quickly in Yoga pants and an old t-shirt. I would change into my baking whites later at the bakery. I always kept my work clothes there so they wouldn't get dirty going back and forth.

Before leaving the house, I grabbed the enormous wicker basket that Sarah had given me just the other week. I was extremely excited to use it because she'd bespelled it to make anything I put in it extremely light and easy to carry.

As I said before, I can hold my own when it comes to lifting heavy things but pears aren't a light fruit and the more of them you have, the harder they are to handle. And since I can only pick from the tree once in an entire year, it's not like I can go back and forth and get more. So what I gather in that one picking is all I have to work with. Which meant for the past few years I'd been breaking my back hauling an enormous heavy basket jam-packed with pears back to my bakery.

Sarah, being a Natural Witch, hadn't even had to do much. When I explained about the problem in gathering the Golden-Skinned Warbler pears, she simply asked what basket I was using. When I pointed it out to her, she touched it and said, "lighter," and that was that.

I couldn't help being a little envious but then, my own witchy powers came naturally to me as well—it just so happened that they all had to do with baking. Sarah's power was much broader but she was so nice about it I couldn't really begrudge her. And of course, I was extremely thankful to have the basket.

I carried the basket—which now weighed almost nothing—down the path that led away from the back of the house my Great Aunt had left me. It ran right along the edge of the magical bubble that enclosed all of Hidden Hollow. As I walked, the white stone walkway glowed faintly in the early morning light.

It wasn't very long before the trees behind my house ended and the path was bordered on the left by a high, wild, evergreen hedge. I didn't know who had planted it, but it was badly in need of a trim. The hedge varied from around the height of my shoulder to a few feet above my head. I had never bothered to try and get around it because it was completely impenetrable and besides, I was happy to stick to the path.

Around a curve I finally came to what I had been looking for—the Golden-Skinned Warbler pear tree. Or at least, *part* of it.

I say part of it because the trunk and most of the limbs of the tree grew on the other side of the hedge. In fact, only a few long branches hung over onto my side. But those few branches produced an enormous amount of fruit when the tree was ready to yield.

To my delight, I saw that my instincts had been right—the branches hanging over the hedge were so heavy with pears that they were dropping nearly down to the ground.

I stared happily at the golden fruit, gleaming in the rays of the rising sun. This was possibly the biggest crop I had ever seen and I could smell the sweet, ripe scent which was like a mixture of pear and honeysuckle long before I got close.

"I knew it!" I exclaimed out loud. I was so happy I did a little dance right there. There were so many pears here! I was going to be able to make so many tarts which I knew would make all of Hidden Hollow happy.

Before I started picking, I took a moment to examine the branches and make my plan of attack. As long as I was actively picking the pears, they would stay good, but the minute I stopped picking for any length of time the pears still attached to the tree would start getting overripe. Eventually they would blacken and shrivel and fall to the ground where they would make a slimy patch on the path and soak into the ground on either side of it. So once I started picking, I had to keep it up continuously until I was done.

As I planned what branch to start on, I couldn't help casting a glance over the top of the hedge to the other side. Many times I had thought about trying to find a way over so I could pick pears over there too, but several things stopped me.

First, I wasn't sure if I could get a huge basket of pears over the top of the extremely prickly hedge which had spiky leaves and inch-long thorns on its branches without hurting myself. And second, I didn't want to go anywhere near the haunted mansion.

No, I'm not talking about the ride at Disney World—"the haunted mansion" was what I called the old dilapidated house I could see on the other side of the hedge. It was an enormous, rundown structure—clearly it had been built for someone or something that wasn't human. Possibly a Troll had once lived there, I thought. Or maybe a Giant? How big did they get, anyway?

I didn't know and didn't want to know. Giants, Trolls, and Ogres are on the list of undesirable Creatures with evil tendencies. Their anti-social natures make it impossible for them to live and mingle with other, more peaceful Creatures and human magic users and I for one wanted nothing to do with them.

So I had long ago decided to ignore that side of the hedge and just gather all the pears I could from the branches that hung over it. And today I had a lot to gather.

Ignoring the broken and boarded up windows of the haunted mansion which seemed to stare at me like blind eyes, I put down my basket in a good spot and started picking.

The pears were humming in the sunshine, their golden skins bursting with juicy goodness. They were so ready to be harvested they practically fell into my hand as I reached for them. Every time one dropped into my palm it let out a musical little *"tra-la!"* as its stem parted from the branch, which let me know that the fruit was indeed perfectly ripe and ready to pick.

I rapidly filled my basket to the brim taking all but one pear—the most beautiful one of all which I was saving for last. In the past, I would have had to leave some pears behind, but now thanks to the bespelled basket, I could carry them all easily back to my bakery.

Humming happily, I picked the very last pear on my side of the hedge and sank my teeth into its golden skin. True, I would be singing for a whole hour after I ate it, but it was totally worth it and besides, I would be working alone in the bakery so it wouldn't matter.

The delicate pear flesh melted on my tongue unlike any other fruit I'd ever had and I took my time eating it. This was probably the only one I would allow myself to eat—all the others were going into the tarts —so I wanted to savor it.

It wasn't until I was down to the core and licking the sticky juice off my fingers that I noticed some movement on the other side of the hedge.

The last bite of pear seemed to stick in my throat as I saw the door of the haunted mansion open and an enormous figure come out of it.

He was hairy all over with a long, greasy, dark orange pelt that covered most of his body. It hung down over the dirty brown shorts he was wearing which appeared to be his only clothing. His head was as big and lumpy as a prize-winning pumpkin and his yellow eyes seemed too small for his face.

I wanted to look away at that point but I couldn't—I felt frozen to the spot and my mind kept cataloging the Creature's lumpy, frightening features. Hairy pointed ears flapped in the breeze and his mouth was filled with long, sharp, curving fangs that seemed to interlock together like the teeth of a bear trap. Overlong arms hung down so low that his knuckles dragged the ground like an ape's as he shambled towards the hedge.

If you're wondering how I could tell for sure that he was male, well it was obvious. There was an enormous, long bulge along the inner thigh of one leg of his shorts. The head of a perfectly huge penis, the size and color of a bruised apple, was hanging out of the shorts, down near his knee. *Disgusting.*

My first thought was that this must be what Bigfoot looked like— only uglier and *way* smellier. Because the breeze was bringing whiffs of his personal odor through the hedge to me and even the sweet aroma of the Golden-Skinned Warbler pears couldn't drown out the rotten stench.

My second thought was that I needed to get away—*fast.*

I didn't think the hairy, smelly Creature—whatever he was—had seen me since I was watching him from behind the hedge. It occurred to me that he might be tall enough to step right over it and I didn't want that. Slowly I picked up my enormous basket—which was still light as a feather, thanks to Sarah's magic—and started walking quickly and quietly back down the path.

I was hoping to get around the curve in the road before he could spot me, but luck wasn't on my side. A moment later I heard a deep angry voice bellow,

"Who's that walking on my path? Who dares to come and wake my wrath?"

Seriously? I couldn't help thinking. But at least his rhyming gave me an idea of what he was—Great Aunt Gertrude had taught me several ways to tell the different Creatures apart. Giants were, of course immensely huge and usually completely bald. And Trolls almost always had more than one head, according to her. Ogres spoke in rhymes. So the hairy, smelly creature behind me must be an Ogre—not that I wanted to hang around long enough to be sure.

After a quick glance over my shoulder to be sure he wasn't following, I sped up my pace and kept walking. But then the Ogre spoke again.

"Girly, I can see you there! Did you come to steal my pears?"

I sped up some more. I was nearly running when I heard the rustling, cracking sound of a huge body breaking through the hedge. Great—he hadn't even bothered to step over it—he'd just crushed his way right through it!

I started running in earnest then, though I still kept a tight grip on my basket. After all, it wasn't heavy at all, so it wasn't slowing me down. I might as well hold on to my valuable harvest of pears—or so I told myself.

I was nearly to the curve in the road when the Ogre spoke a third time—and this time his words had power in them.

"By the laws that bind us all, I bid you now to stop and stall!" he roared from behind me.

His roar shattered the early morning quiet and the birds which had been singing in the nearby trees suddenly fell silent. I tried to keep going and ignore him but, to my horror, I found that my footsteps were slowing. Suddenly it was like I was moving in slow motion, with every step getting harder and harder to take. And every minute I could hear the Ogre getting closer.

I dared to turn my head again and saw that he was only a few paces behind me. His long greasy hair was whipping in the wind and his putrid scent, like unwashed genitals and rotten garbage left in the sun, was suddenly all around me. His long, curving jaws were open and I could see a horribly long, red tongue behind them, reaching out as though he wanted to taste me!

I opened my mouth and screamed for help—only because I had eaten a Golden Warbler pear, I *sang* it instead.

"Help!" I cried and it came out sounding almost operatic—like a soprano singing a high note.

The Ogre let out a grating laugh.

"No use to cry, you'll soon be dead. I'll grind your bones to make my bread!"

My heart was pounding as though I was running a marathon but my feet were now stuck to the ground as though someone had super-glued the soles of my sneakers to the stones of the path.

I could feel myself starting to hyperventilate. Oh God, was I really going to die here and now? Aunt Gertrude had tried to warn me about evil Creatures—she'd told me I shouldn't wander too far from the house near the edges of the magical bubble that surrounded the town. But I hadn't listened to her and now I was going to pay. This was the end—the Ogre was going to bite my head right off my shoulders! Or else he would literally tear me limb-from-limb. He would—

There was a rushing sound in my ears and suddenly Malik was there, right beside me. He was dressed less formally than he had been last night, in jeans and t-shirt that strained over his broad chest, but I barely had time to notice his clothes.

Before I knew it, the Incubus was putting himself between me and the Ogre and glaring menacingly up at my would-be attacker.

"Get back!" he growled, his voice deep and menacing. "And remove the spell you cast on my woman!"

I was able to turn my head enough to see the Ogre scowl at his words.

"If she's your woman, take control! She trespassed on my ground and stole!" he declared.

"No, I didn't!" I said but again my words came out in song—a squeaky, high, frightened melody that was in all minor keys, probably because I was still scared to death. I appreciated Malik standing up for me, but the Ogre was taller than the Incubus by several feet and his big, meaty fists looked capable of crushing a person's skull with one blow.

"She stole, she stole! Look at her bowl!" the Ogre insisted.

"If you mean her basket, I don't see any problem," Malik said coolly. "She was simply harvesting fruit."

"My fruit she took! Just take a look!" the Ogre grated.

"I've been picking pears from that tree for years," I sang. "He never claimed them before and besides, I only picked from…from the branches hanging over the hedge."

My voice was starting to wobble because I was still so afraid. Also, the Ogre's scent was nauseating. I just wanted to get away from him but my shoes were still stuck to the path. And what if Malik decided to just give up and let the Ogre have me? I didn't know the Incubus well enough to know if I could trust him to stand by me or not.

But despite my doubt Malik stood his ground.

"You heard the lady," he said firmly. "She only took fruit from this side of the hedge—you don't own the path. It's not on your property."

"But the tree belongs to me!" the Ogre declared.

"I don't give a fuck," Malik growled, clearly losing patience. "Now are you going to take your stasis spell off her or am I going to *make* you do it?"

As he spoke, his eyes began to glow with a Hellish light and he seemed to increase in stature. His shoulders got even broader and he was suddenly a head taller and even more muscular. The sharp points of his curving horns gleamed in the sunlight and even his tail looked ready to attack. It hovered in the air beside him like a cobra about to strike.

The Ogre stared at the Incubus uncertainly. He was still taller but despite his size, he was clearly mostly flab and hair. If it came to a fight, I didn't know who would win but I thought even if Malik lost he would make the other Creature pay dearly in the process.

The Ogre must have thought the same thing because at last I felt the magical grip on my legs loosening. He pointed one finger with a long, dirty fingernail at Malik and me.

"For now go free, but you will see that you can run but we're not done!"

Malik glared at him.

"Stay away from my woman," he growled. "If you threaten her again, you'll be picking your teeth out of your asshole because I'll fucking turn you inside out you hairy bastard! Oh, and take a bath— you smell like sewage."

Then he put an arm around me and urged me forward on the path.

I found that I could move my feet again and I set off at a steady trot, still clutching the basket of pears. I dared to toss one quick look over my shoulder, only because Malik was at my side. What I saw wasn't exactly comforting. The Ogre was staring at me with a look of such hatred it made my blood run cold.

Hatred and something else. Was it…hunger?

As he saw me looking, the long red tongue I had seen behind the curving daggers of his teeth shot out and licked sloppily around his thick, rubbery lips.

I felt my stomach turn over queasily and I turned quickly away. But I couldn't get that hungry expression out of my head or forget how close I had come to dying right there on the path behind my house.

CHAPTER NINE

Somehow I waited until I got in the door of my house to break down.

Please don't misunderstand—I'm not the kind of woman who cries easily or often but having a near brush with death will puncture anyone's cool. And I had no illusions about what the Ogre wanted to do to me.

You know all those fairytales where the innocent children get eaten by the monster? Well, they're popular for a reason. Back before there was a barrier between the Creature World and the Mortal Realm, children actually *did* get eaten by monsters—or Creatures with evil tendencies. Those fairytales were there to warn people not to get too close to the dark side of magic that lurked in the gloomy heart of the forest or the silent caves deep under the mountains.

People see the old stories as fiction now, but there's a kernel of truth in every single one of them. Evil Creatures really *do* hunger for human flesh and drink human blood when they can get it. That's why they can't be trusted to live in a town like Hidden Hollow where Creatures and human magic users intermingle.

So yes, as soon as I got into the house with the door shut behind me, I started crying because I'd had a near death experience and part of me was certain I was still in danger.

"Hey, hey, it's all right. Come on now, put these down." Malik carefully extracted the basket of pears, which I was holding in a death grip, from my grasp and put it down on the kitchen table. Then he looked down at me anxiously. "It's all right now, Celia. Everything will be fine."

"N-no it won't!" I sang-cried. (And if you've never heard anyone sing while they were crying, all I can say is that it sounds really strange.) "W-what if he comes to the house?"

"He won't—this house is well warded," Malik assured me. "Believe me, I wouldn't have been able to get in myself if you hadn't opened the door to Goody Albright and let her bring my portrait inside."

His words calmed me somewhat—I had forgotten about the magical wards around the house that Great Aunt Gertrude had put in place. Honestly, I had never had to think of them before because I'd never had an evil Creature come after me.

"I thought…thought he would kill me or eat me or both!" I sang-cried, swiping at my streaming eyes.

"I'm sure he'd like to try, but no one is getting anywhere near you while I'm here," Malik said grimly. "I might have been too late to save Hester, but I'm here for you." He pulled me against his chest and wrapped his arms around me. "Take some deep breaths, baby—you're safe now. I promise."

Though I told myself I still didn't know him—not outside my dreams anyway—being held against his broad, warm chest was comforting. As I breathed in his smoke and spice scent, I felt my heart rate slowing and my breathing evening out. I had a deep, primal feeling that I was in the arms of a man who would kill or die to protect me—if Demons could die, that was—and somehow that calmed me down most of all.

"That's right, just breathe," Malik rumbled, rubbing my back and shoulders soothingly. "Just relax and tell me all about it—tell me what happened."

"Do I have to?" I sang in a low voice, looking up at him. The whole incident had been so nasty and viscerally frightening I just wanted to forget it.

But Malik gave me a stern look.

"I'm afraid you do. I need to know everything so I can protect you."

Part of me—the independent part who owned her own business—wanted to protest that I didn't need protection. Luckily the sensible part of me recognized that I absolutely did.

Taking a deep breath, I told him everything—singing sadly in a minor key about the pear tree and how it only bore fruit once a year and how I always harvested it and made tarts for the whole town.

"I didn't think anyone lived in the haunted mansion—the old house on the other side of the hedge," I sang. "But I guess the Ogre must and I just never saw him before."

"Not necessarily—he might just be squatting there," Malik said, looking thoughtful. "At any rate, the pears are in your house now and possession is nine-tenths of Creature Law so they're yours now and he can't do anything about it."

"Thank you for coming to save me," I sang softly, looking up at him. "I don't know how to thank you."

"Well, I *would* say you could let me fulfill your deepest fantasy so I could be free of the Mortal Realm and go back to my rightful place in Hell's Waiting Room, but I think that would be in poor taste right now. So I'll settle for helping you turn those luscious pears into delicious tarts."

"You want to help me bake?" I sang doubtfully. I had never trusted anyone but Sarah in my bakery before now and that was only after I gave her a thorough trial. She had the day off today because she'd covered the entire bakery by herself on my birthday, but I wasn't sure if I wanted Malik's help—who even knew if he knew how to bake?

But he didn't seem fazed by my doubt.

"Sure, why not?" he said, smiling down at me. "Baking is your gift and I want to learn more about you. Only so I can learn what your fantasy is and fulfill it, of course," he added quickly.

"Oh, of course." I sighed and even my sigh sounded musical. "I guess you can help but you have to do what I say. Pastry is easy to ruin if you don't know what you're doing."

"Don't worry—I'm a fast learner." Malik winked and then he leaned down and kissed me on the forehead. "I just want to spend time with you," he murmured, searching my eyes with his own. "I don't care what we do as long as we do it *together*."

My heart gave a little jump in my chest. It was exactly the kind of thing I'd always wished a man would say to me.

Exactly, whispered a little voice in my head. *And that's why he's saying it. He's here to fulfill your fantasies and not all of them are sexual, right?*

Right. I told myself not to trust the Incubus's words—he was, after all, a Demon. And there was no way I could trust my heart to a lust Demon—someone who actually made women fall in love with them for a living. I was just another job to him—an unfulfilled obligation due to the fact that I had Hester's blood in my veins.

But no matter how I scolded myself, I couldn't help liking the way he was looking at me, or remembering how good it felt to be held in his arms.

CHAPTER TEN

"Now I know you're worried that I don't know how to bake and that I'll ruin your tarts," Malik announced once we were both in the bakery with the pears washed and laid out on clean cloths on the counter of my workspace in the back of the bakery.

"What? I never said that," I protested uneasily. (Luckily the effects of the pear I'd eaten had finally worn off so I was talking, not singing.)

"No, but you were thinking it back at your house when I was holding you," he said firmly. "But I want you to know there's a way to calm your fears and be sure I don't fuck things up."

"Oh? And how is that?" I asked, frowning.

"You just have to let me kiss you."

"What? *Come on,*" I exclaimed. "You're not serious!"

"Yes, I am," Malik said patiently. "You know I can hear what you're thinking when I touch you. Well, another demonic skill of mine is the ability to pick up new skills and information when I touch a mortal long enough and intimately enough."

"You're not serious," I said skeptically.

"Yes, I am," he insisted.

"So you can pick up all my baking knowledge just by kissing me?"

His black eyes went heavy-lidded.

"Well, I *could* eat your luscious little pussy instead, if you'd prefer it."

My heart was suddenly thudding in my chest and I felt my cheeks getting hot.

"No! I mean, that's not…I don't want…"

"Yes, you do, baby," he growled softly, taking me in his arms. "That's *definitely* one of your fantasies. Getting your pussy eaten by a man who knows how to do it—and who *wants* to do it. But for now, I'll settle for a kiss."

Before I could protest again, his mouth found mine and I was drowning in a sweet, hot kiss that stole my breath and made my whole body ache with desire.

His lips were insistent but he didn't ram his tongue down my throat, like some other guys I'd been with. Instead he teased me, kissing me softly but urgently, then probing lightly with just the tip of his tongue at the seam of my lips.

I opened to him with a little moan and his tongue darted in to dance with mine before withdrawing as he sucked lightly at the tip, inviting me to explore him the way he had explored me.

I took his invitation without thinking, slipping my tongue eagerly between his lips and tasting him in turn. His mouth was hot and he tasted inexplicably and deliciously like cinnamon candy.

I don't know how long the kiss went on for—I never wanted it to end. It was hands down the most erotic kiss of my life and it sent shivers of desire through my whole body. My nipples were tight little peaks inside my baker's whites and my pussy was suddenly liquid with desire. My clit, where he had stung me with his tail earlier, was throbbing like a second heartbeat between my legs and my mind was filled with all kinds of erotic images.

I saw myself naked on the couch with Malik kneeling in front of me, his face buried between my legs as I gripped his horns and urged him on…I saw him taking me from behind, bending me over the metal counter of my bakery workspace, gripping my hips as he plunged into me and I moaned and backed to meet every thrust…I saw the two of us in bed with me on top, riding him as I gasped and rolled my hips, taking him in deeper and deeper…

And then, just as I was thinking I might come just from all the mental pornography and kissing alone, he pulled back, ending the kiss.

"Oh!" I half gasped/half moaned as I looked up at him. "That was…why did you stop?"

He gave me a grin that was full of lazy lust.

"Because I got all the information I needed. And because we need to get baking—don't we?"

"Oh, I…I guess we do." I nodded, still feeling dizzy with lust and the aftermath of the kiss. My body was humming with desire and I wished for a moment that I could just give in and go for it right there with the big Incubus. But no, I wasn't going to do that. I had a bakery to run and pear tarts to make. Malik was right—we had to get down to business.

And so we did. I already had a lot of puff pastry in my refrigerator unit that I'd laminated earlier in the week. I'd had a feeling that the pears were going to be ripe soon and I wanted to be ready. So what I mainly had to do was roll out the dough, cut and prep the pears, put the tarts together and bake them. And to my surprise, Malik worked along side me with ease and competence.

The big Incubus seemed to know exactly what to do—I barely had to show him anything. It was like working with Sarah, who was also a natural baker.

It was also nice how strong he was. I was used to working with huge blobs of dough and the enormous metal mixing bowl of my industrial sized mixer, but it always took some effort on my part. Malik didn't even have to try—when I ran out of pre-made dough and decided to make another batch, he lifted the bowl and turned the dough out onto the work area without even breaking a sweat. I loved watching his muscles flex as he did it too—he looked amazingly hot in the plain white t-shirt and white baker's trousers he had conjured for himself to wear.

I had put out the "Pear Tarts Later Today" sign that a thoughtful customer had made me last year on the front door, so nobody bothered us as we worked. I had always made the tarts alone in the past but I found I liked having help. It made everything go so much faster having Malik beside me—even if I *did* keep having intrusive thoughts about letting him touch me and taste me.

I was pretty sure that Malik was sending me some of those thoughts. Every time he brushed past me or touched my arm or hand when he handed me something I got another mental image of all the hot and dirty things he wanted to do to me. I would have told him to stop it, but I confess I was kind of enjoying it. It made me feel desired to look up from cutting out another row of tarts and see the big Incubus staring at me with heat in his eyes. I had to blush and look away, but I couldn't help loving the feeling that he wanted me so much.

He doesn't really want you—he's just pretending. It's just his job, whispered a skeptical little voice in my head. But I didn't really believe it. Malik wasn't acting—he'd been as into that kiss as I was. Besides, I could almost *smell* his lust in the air—mingling with my own. It was like we were creating a brand-new fragrance together that was all about longing and desire.

"We stopped for a brief lunch—sandwiches that I'd made the day before and left in the fridge—and then worked into the afternoon. At around two o'clock I was finally ready to open the doors.

"All right, do you want to run the register or wrap up the tarts?" I asked him as we got ready to let in the crowd that was already forming.

"Whichever you want me to do," Malik said, smiling. We'd both been working hard all day but he wasn't grumpy like a lot of men get. He still had a charming smile which I felt right down to my toes when he turned it on me.

"You'd better let me run the register," I said, laughing. "If I let you do it, every female resident of Hidden Hollow is going to forget their own name and what they came in for the minute they see you."

"I don't think anyone can forget what they came in for." He inhaled deeply. "The tarts smell *amazing*—which is probably why you already have so many customers lined up outside."

I looked at the line outside the bakery and sighed.

"Yeah, well I hope they like this year's tarts because there aren't going to be any more."

Malik frowned.

"Why do you say that?"

"Well, because—the Ogre. Mr. Grimy Rhymey," I said dryly. "If the Golden Warbler pear tree really does belong to him, I can't take anymore pears. And even if it doesn't, I'm never going to risk going back there again!" I shivered at the thought.

"Don't get ahead of yourself," Malik counseled. "If you've never seen him before in all the years you've been walking on that path and picking the pears, chances are he's just *saying* he owns the—what did you call it? Oh, right—the 'haunted mansion—' and the pear tree."

"Maybe you're right," I said. "But I'm still not going to risk going back there again. If you hadn't come out to save me just when you did—"

"Don't think about it." He put a hand on my shoulder and squeezed gently. "Think about this instead." And he leaned down to give me a lingering kiss on the lips that sent sparks of desire shooting through my body and planted another naughty scene in my mind—the two of us holding each other naked in bed, looking into each other's eyes as he—

"Hey—when are you going to open?" a voice shouted from outside.

"Oops, I'd better go let them in," I told Malik, pulling away. "Get ready—it's going to be crowded for a while."

"We can handle it together," he murmured, giving me another smile. "And afterwards maybe we can talk some more about fulfilling that fantasy of yours."

"Maybe…" I said noncommittally. I had to confess that I wasn't nearly so resistant to letting him fulfill some of my sexual fantasies now. The way he had defended me from the Ogre had been wonderful but the way he'd pitched in and worked beside me, helping me instead of expecting me to do everything, was almost as good.

Did I mention that I dated a lot of mama's boys before I gave up on the dating apps? It was so nice to meet a man who acted like an adult and actually wanted to help me and fulfill my needs instead of expecting me to take care of him and do everything myself.

Better slow down there, Celia, whispered the pessimistic voice in my head. *Remember, he's not a guy you're dating—he's a lust Demon who's only interested in fulfilling the contract he had with your ancestress so he can be free and go back to Hell's Waiting Room. So the minute you let him get really intimate with you, he'll be gone. It's better not to let your heart get involved.*

That was true, I reluctantly admitted to myself. Even if I did get physical with the delicious Demon—and believe me, after having an entire day of teasing and erotic mental images, I definitely wanted to—I would have to be careful not to let myself catch feelings.

I would have pondered more on the subject but at that moment Malik opened the door and the customers started pouring in so I couldn't think about anything else but serving everyone in town.

CHAPTER ELEVEN

I think everyone in Hidden Hollow stopped by your bakery today," Malik remarked, dropping onto the faded floral print couch in my living room with a sigh. Even for an immortal Demon, he looked tired.

"You're right about that," I said, settling beside him. "Every year I make the tarts, they get more popular. I can't believe we sold out in an hour!"

I'd actually had to put a limit of two tarts per customer, because people wanted to buy a dozen at a time. Of course I had saved some back for Goldie to serve at her diner and some for Goody Albright to serve with the High Tea she advertised at her B&B but all the rest had gone to hungry repeat customers and people who had just moved to town and had heard about the tarts from their new neighbors.

Luckily we'd cleaned the bakery *before* opening the doors so after the last tart was sold, I was able to close up shop and go home early for the day. But of course, none of that would have been possible without Malik's help. In the past, when I did tart day all by myself, I sometimes didn't get home until nearly midnight. But there was still light in the sky as we walked through the crisp Fall weather from The Lost Lamb back to my house.

But even though it hadn't lasted nearly as long as last year's tart day, it had still been a long day. My feet were aching and I was glad to get off them and prop my feet up on the ugly brown coffee table that Great Aunt Gertrude had left me. She had terrible taste in furniture but I hadn't had the heart to get rid of her stuff and get stuff of my own when I moved in to the old Victorian mansion. I wasn't much of an interior decorator and I was always busy baking. When did I have time to furniture shop?

"You look tired," Malik remarked, turning his head to look at me. There was concern in his black eyes.

"So do you," I countered. "Only I didn't know immortal Demons could *get* tired."

"I expend energy the same way you do when I take corporeal form," he remarked. "It's not like living in spirit form where you *are* energy."

"Is that what everyone is down there in, uh, Hell's Waiting Room?" I asked with interest. "Pure energy?"

"Something like that." He scooted closer to me and smiled. "But I don't mind getting tired if it means I get to spend time with you."

"Don't talk like that," I said, looking away. "Don't talk like you know me and really want to spend time with me—you don't."

"Yes, I *do* know you," he protested. "We've been meeting in your dreams for the past six months. And of course I want to spend time with you—it was your longing that brought me out of deep slumber and woke me completely."

"Well...I don't know if that counts," I mumbled, looking down at my hands. "I barely remember those dreams."

But I was lying—the dreams I'd forgotten had been coming back to me in bits and pieces. Almost all of them were erotic but in some of them Malik and I just talked and got to know each other. I had to admit, I probably knew the big Incubus better than I did many of the men I'd dated in the past. Which didn't make it any easier to sit right beside him when I was still feeling the lingering desire that had been teasing me all day long.

"You remember," Malik murmured. Reaching out, he cupped my cheek and turned me face up to his. "I think you remember very well, Celia."

He took my mouth in a kiss and I have to confess, I didn't try to stop him. Despite the long day we'd both had, I could feel his energy flowing through me. It was like he was a power source that I had somehow plugged in to and he was charging my battery—in more ways than one.

"*Mmm*," he murmured, breaking the kiss at last. "What about that fantasy now? How about if I fulfill it?"

I bit my lip, looking up at him uncertainly.

"If I let you do that though, doesn't it mean you'll go away? I mean, what if that Ogre comes back again. I know my house is warded against evil Creatures but—"

"Ah, I see what's worrying you," he murmured. "What if I promised not to leave you until the situation with the Ogre is resolved?"

"Really?" I looked at him hopefully. "You'd do that?"

"Of course!" His handsome face grew serious. "I told you before, I wasn't in time to save Hester. I have an obligation to your bloodline—I won't leave before I fulfill it."

I looked away.

"So that's the reason you're staying? Just to fulfill an obligation?"

"No, I'm staying because I *want* to. Because over the last six months we've been dreaming of each other, I realized what a unique woman you are, Celia. And that I want to get to know you better—*much* better."

I started to answer, but he took my mouth again in a much more passionate and urgent kiss this time. I couldn't help myself—I gave in and kissed him back. I let my hands wander over his broad chest and breathed in his warm, smoke and spice scent as the two of us kissed each other hungrily and deeply.

But Malik wasn't content just to taste my mouth. A moment later, he broke the kiss. Before I could protest, he brushed my hair away from my neck and began to kiss me there, too, nibbling and flicking his tongue over the sensitive skin to send pleasure racing through my whole body.

My neck has always been an erogenous zone for me. The minute he started kissing me there, I felt my body reacting. My nipples got so tight they almost hurt and my pussy was suddenly wet and hot. My clit was throbbing again and I shifted on the couch, wondering vaguely if it had anything to do with the way he had stung me with his tail when he had first appeared in my bed.

"*Mmm*, as a matter of fact, that's *exactly* what's happening," Malik murmured against my neck.

"Uh, what?" I panted, barely able to concentrate.

Malik looked up, his eyes half-lidded.

"The aching you feel in your sweet little clit is a result of my venom," he said.

"Your venom?" My eyes got wide, though I couldn't get *too* upset— I was too turned on for that.

"Yes, my venom," he repeated and suddenly his tail was hovering just in my line of sight. "In small quantities it brings intense pleasure and sensitivity. Watch…"

And before I could protest, he reached into my t-shirt and bra and pulled out one of my breasts. Before I could stop him, the end of his tail was curling around my breast while the pointed tip teased lightly at my tight nipple.

"Hey," I protested breathlessly. "Don't really sting me, okay?"

"Why not? It doesn't have to hurt—you just weren't prepared for it last time," he said. "Now you know what's coming, you should feel only pleasure."

"But—" I began but then the tip of his tail suddenly pressed directly against my nipple.

I expected to feel a sharp stinging sensation but, as Malik had promised there wasn't even a pinch or any pain at all. Instead, I felt a sensation of intense pleasure—almost like I was having an orgasm through my nipple, if that makes any sense.

"Oh!" I gasped, writhing on the couch.

"See? It feels good, doesn't it?" Malik gave me a devilish smile. "And see how much more sensitive your nipple is now?"

Looking down, I could see that the nipple he had stung was indeed looking more sensitive. It was darker and larger than it had been—almost as though it was swollen with pleasure.

"Look, let's do a comparison." Reaching into my shirt again, Malik pulled out my other breast. Holding my eyes with his the whole time, he leaned forward and captured my un-stung nipple in his mouth.

I moaned breathlessly as he circled my nipple with his tongue. It felt *really* good. I've always liked having my breasts and nipples played with—as long as the guy knows what he's doing—and the big Incubus *definitely* did.

Reluctantly, I thought, he let my nipple slip from his lips.

"That was nice, wasn't it?" he murmured.

I nodded mutely. It had been a whole lot more than just "nice."

"But see how much better it feels when I sting you first," Malik went on.

Leaning down again, he took my other nipple—the one he'd stung with his tail—between his lips and began to tease it exactly the same way.

I nearly jumped out of my skin! The pleasure of his hot mouth enveloping me and his talented tongue swirling around my swollen peak was multiplied exponentially. I gasped and grabbed for his horns, but I didn't know if I was trying to push him away...or pull him closer.

"Oh! Oh my God—Malik!" I moaned, thrusting my chest out to offer him more. "Oh, that feels so good but I think I'm going to... going to come if you don't stop!"

He pulled back at last, giving me a knowing smile.

"And do you *want* to come like this, Celia?" he murmured. "Or would you rather come with my mouth between your thighs?"

I felt myself going hot all over. How could he know how I had always fantasized about a man going down on me?

"Because I'm touching you, of course," he murmured, answering my silent question. "So I know how you long to have a man between your thighs who knows what he's doing—just as I know that every man you've ever let try tasting you has been a disappointment in some way."

He was definitely right about that. Every time I let a guy go down on me—and there hadn't been many—it was almost like they were afraid of my pussy. They gave a few hesitant licks and then gave up. The one time I had a guy between my legs who actually showed any enthusiasm, he latched onto an area that was nowhere near my clit. I had tried to redirect him but he kept going back to that one spot until I finally gave up and tapped him on the shoulder to let him know I'd had enough.

It had gotten to the point where I believed getting oral sex was one of those things it's amazing to fantasize about but almost always disappointing to experience in real life. I wasn't sure if anyone could really change my mind about that.

"I can," Malik rumbled confidently. "And I can find your sweet little clit, too. But just in case you need to redirect me, I have natural handles for you right here." He tapped one of his horns and gave me a knowing, half-lidded smile.

"Oh…" I bit my lip. I really wanted to let him do this, but I still felt a little shy about it. "Maybe…maybe I should take a shower first," I said hesitantly.

"No—I want to taste you just like you are," he growled. "Now pull down your panties and let me see that sweet pussy."

He was already working on pulling down my yoga pants, which I had changed back into before we went home. The way he was looking at me coupled with his commanding tone turned me to liquid from the waist down. With a little gasp I raised my hips to help him strip down the pants and panties, baring me completely.

"Good girl," Malik growled and he was already on the floor and spreading my legs . "Now just relax and let me taste that sweet pussy."

"Are…are you going to sting me again?" I panted.

He looked up.

"Do you *want* me to sting you?"

I bit my lip.

"I…I don't know."

"Why don't you watch this and think about it then."

And then the triangular end of his tail was suddenly there, teasing lightly around the curls that grew on my mound and then tracing the slit of my pussy with its tip.

"Oh!" I moaned softly as the tail dipped deeper, sliding into my wet folds to caress my aching clit.

"*Mmm*, look at that sweet little clit," Malik murmured. Leaning forward, he parted my outer lips with his thumbs, opening me for his tail.

I watched, mesmerized, as it teased me, sliding around and around the sensitive little button and making me moan again with the intense pleasure. I kept expecting him to sting me, but he didn't—I wondered why not.

"Because I want the pleasure of tasting you and making you come with my mouth and tongue first," Malik growled, answering my question. "I'll sting you again but right now I can't wait to eat that sweet, creamy pussy. Spread wider, baby—let me in."

And with that, he leaned all the way forward this time and captured my aching clit between his lips.

I was still somewhat sensitive from the first time he'd stung me, so I moaned and jerked, my hips bucking involuntarily as he licked me. My reaction seemed to please Malik because I heard a low rumble of approval in his throat and then he was pressing forward and licking me in earnest.

I had never had a guy go down on me like this before—with such a mixture of enthusiasm and skill. He seemed to know exactly what to do and how to taste me to bring me maximum pleasure. And more than that, he seemed to really be *enjoying* what he was doing.

Malik looked up for a moment, his mouth shiny with my juices.

"Of course I'm enjoying it—I fucking *love* eating your pussy, sweetheart. Knew I would. Spread wider—going to make you come."

I moaned and did as he commanded. As soon as I obeyed, he started licking me like I was his favorite flavor ice cream in the world and I was in danger of melting.

I definitely *was* in danger of melting. Hardly knowing what I was doing, I gripped his horns in my hands and held on tight while I bucked up to meet the hot tongue invading my pussy.

Malik seemed to love his. He growled deep in his throat and his long, muscular arms wound around my thighs, splitting me even wider as he buried his face between them. It was like tasting me was more than just pleasing to him—it was like he *needed* to do it—like he was so hungry for me he couldn't stop himself and there was nothing he would rather be doing at that exact moment.

"Malik...*Malik!*" I found I was chanting his name like a prayer as I pressed forward to meet him. He had found my special spot—the right side of my aching clit—and was licking it over and over again, pushing me higher and higher until I was sure I was about to explode. If only I could have just a little more stimulation...

Again, the big Incubus knew exactly what I needed. I felt the tip of his tail slipping inside me and at first I was afraid he might sting me. But then I felt it swelling to fill me as he found the end of my channel. Oh God, it was getting so big inside me! My inner walls were stretching to take him but it felt *good*—it felt like exactly what I needed to finally come.

Sure enough, being licked and filled at the same time was more than I could stand. I gave a low cry as I felt my orgasm rushing through me. My back arched and I grabbed his horns so hard I was sure I would have marks on my hands later—not that I cared.

"Malik!" I moaned loudly. "Oh my God, yes—please! Don't stop! Right there—don't stop!"

He didn't stop. In fact, he lapped even harder, riding out my orgasm as I tugged hard on his horns and his tail swelled inside me until I couldn't take it anymore.

"Oh!" I panted. "Oh please…too much…too much!"

Malik didn't stop licking at once, but his tongue became gentler and he began licking all around my clit instead of focusing on it exclusively.

I moaned softly as his tail slipped out of my pussy. I watched in wonder as it went from a thick club back to a thin whip and the end of it, which had become a rounded head, turned back into a triangle.

"I…I didn't know you could do that with…with your tail," I panted, finally letting go of his horns. "I mean, change its shape like that or making it bigger and smaller."

He licked his lips and looked up at me with half-lidded eyes.

"Fucking delicious. There's a lot you don't know about me, baby."

"*Mmm…*" I reached for his horns again and pulled him towards me.

Malik rose up on his knees and captured my mouth in a kiss. I moaned and opened my lips for him, loving my own secret flavor on his tongue.

I think we would have gone for it right then and there on my Great Aunt's couch if there hadn't been a sudden pounding on my front door.

"Oh!" I gasped as we pulled apart. "Who could that be?"

My question was answered almost immediately as I heard Goody Albright's voice calling,

"Celia? Can you please come out? We have a rather large problem!"

CHAPTER TWELVE

I hurriedly pulled on my clothes and ran for the front door. When I pulled it open, I saw Goody Albright standing there, looking more upset than I had ever seen her. Her usually neatly coiffed gray hair was all askew, as though she'd been raking her hands through it. And her sharp green eyes, behind her gold-rimmed spectacles, looked nearly wild.

"Goody Albright? What's wrong?" I exclaimed. "Is the Red Lion on fire?"

"As a matter of fact it *is*—only not how you're thinking." She grabbed me by the arm. "Come on—I need to show you something."

"What? What is it?" I demanded, nearly running to keep up with her. But Goody Albright wouldn't answer—she just kept dragging me in the direction of Main Street, where all the businesses of Hidden Hollow were located.

Malik was right behind us and I threw a worried look over my shoulder at him. He shrugged in obvious confusion but I was glad he was with me anyway. Whatever it was Goody Albright wanted to show me, it didn't seem good and I was glad to have someone backing me up.

Since we were practically running—Goody Albright could really move when she wanted to—we got to the Red Lion pretty quickly.

"There." Goody Albright stopped in front of the broad front porch which extended the entire length of her B&B and flung out an arm.

For a moment, I wasn't quite sure what was going on. It was twilight and the lighting was very dim. There were no flames shooting out of the windows of the bed and breakfast though there *did* seem to be an unusually large number of people on the front porch. They seemed to be doing something, but what? I squinted and took a few steps forward.

Then I heard a low groan and someone gasped in a musical voice,

"That's right—give it to me, Sherman! Oh Goddess, that feels so *good!*"

"Oh my!" I breathed, putting a hand to my mouth as I finally realized what was going on. "They're…"

"They're all up there *fucking*. Please excuse my language," Goody Albright said tartly. "All of my guests—do you know who they are, Celia?"

"Er, no. Sorry." I shrugged uncertainly. "Who are they?"

"This week the Red Lion is hosting The Council of Wisdom—an assembly of elder witches and warlocks who are the oldest and most esteemed members of the magical community. They travel around the world, judging the most difficult cases in the magical court system. They are revered for their wisdom and restraint!" Goody Albright went on. "Not a single one of them is under five hundred years old. And now just *look* at them!"

I bit my lip. My eyes had adjusted to the gloom and I could see that an extremely elderly orgy was happening on the Red Lion's front porch. No wonder Goody Albright was upset! The scene reminded me of something, but I couldn't quite place what it was…

"I see that they're, er, getting busy," I said to her. "But what does it have to do with me?"

"Well, remember how I came into The Lost Lamb earlier to get the tarts you'd promised to hold back for me?" she asked, raising her eyebrows.

"Yes?" I said, making it a question.

"Well, I fed them to my guests as a special treat during their sunset and stargazing assembly—they're *supposed* to be watching the evening stars come out right now. I even gave up my own tart so that everyone could have one," she said. "And not long after they finished them, *this* started!"

She gestured again to the porch where a lot of vigorous thrusting and musical moaning was going on. Because of course since they'd all eaten the Golden Warbler tarts, they were all singing instead of speaking. It was a sexual, musical, geriatric mess up there!

"Are you saying my *tarts* did this to them?" I protested. "But I never..."

I trailed off because I had suddenly remembered what the scene reminded me of—it looked an awful lot like the Pilgrim orgy Malik had shown me in his memories of what had happened to Hester, my ancestress, after everyone ate her gooseberry pie.

"Oh, no!" I exclaimed. "But how is this possible? I didn't do anything on purpose!"

"I'm afraid this is my fault," Malik said, stepping forward.

"And who might *you* be?" Goody Albright frowned up at him. "You look familiar—are you the Demon in the portrait I gave to Celia?"

"I am. She freed me from it," he said, nodding. "I am Malik, professional Incubus at your service." He took Goody Albright's hand and bowed over it gallantly, but she snatched it back at once.

"Well, Malik, if this is your doing, you have a lot to answer for! These witches and warlocks are extremely old and fragile—their bones are brittle! I'll be lucky if I don't have to call Madam Healer for the whole lot of them once this is over."

"Forgive me," Malik said sincerely. "I helped Celia make the pear tarts and I'm afraid the fact that I was, er, stimulating her mentally caused her magic to manifest in her baking."

I thought of how horny I'd been the whole time we were making the tarts—because every time he touched me, I got dirty images of the two of us going at it in different ways.

"It's the same thing that happened to Hester," I muttered. "My longing and desire went into the tarts the same way hers went into her gooseberry pie!"

"Since you now appear to know what happened, do you have an antidote?" Goody Albright asked me. "I hate to blame you, dear, but this is probably happening all over town," she added. "I do believe *everyone* in Hidden Hollow ate at least one of your tarts!"

"I'm afraid you're right. God!" I put my hands to my face. "I'm so sorry! I never meant for this to happen!"

"I take it that means you *don't* have an antidote then?" Goody Albright asked unhappily.

"The only cure for unrequited longing and lust is to be with the one you love. Or the one you lust for," Malik said. "I'm afraid this will simply have to run its course."

"Run its course? But how long will *that* take?" Goody Albright demanded.

He shrugged.

"Until the ones affected are fully satiated." He looked at me. "I'm truly sorry, Celia."

"Sorry? You're *sorry?*" I exploded as the full impact of what was happening sank in. Right now, this very minute, everyone in Hidden Hollow who had eaten one of the Golden Warbler tarts was singing their heads off and fucking their brains out! The whole town was one big orgy and as far as they knew, it was *all my fault!*

"Do you realize what this means? I'm finished in this town! Nobody is ever going to want to eat anything I bake ever again!" I yelled at Malik.

Malik held his hands out in a "don't shoot" gesture.

"I swear to you, Celia, I never meant for this to happen. I don't—"

"No, stop talking to me." I put up a hand to stop him. "I don't want to hear anymore. Just go."

"But your deepest fantasy—" he began.

"My deepest fantasy is to never see *you* again!" I snapped.

The minute the words were out of my mouth, part of me regretted them. But it was too late to take them back.

Malik's handsome face went cold and he nodded stiffly.

"Very well. Then I'll consider the business between us closed."

"Good!" I snapped, still too sore and upset to stop myself.

"Fine. I'll be going then."

"All right—go!" I made a gesture at him.

"Have a nice life, Celia," he said coldly.

And then he vanished in a puff of smoke.

CHAPTER THIRTEEN

I managed to hold back my tears until I got home but the moment the door closed behind me, I started sobbing. I was sure my life in Hidden Hollow was ruined—after all, who was ever going to trust me again after this? They were all probably going to assume that I had dumped a lust potion into the pear filling on purpose before making the tarts. I had basically given the whole town a magical aphrodisiac that would have them humping for hours!

But if I was being honest, it wasn't just my shattered reputation and ruined business I was crying for. I couldn't help missing Malik, even though I told myself I shouldn't. This was all his fault, after all. If he hadn't made me so horny while we were making the tarts, my magic never would have seeped into them to poison the whole town with unrequited lust! And besides, I hadn't even known him for a whole twenty-four hours when he left. He'd literally been with me for less than one day—losing him should be no big deal.

It didn't seem to matter what I told myself though—I couldn't stop thinking about the big Incubus—couldn't stop remembering how he'd saved me from the Ogre and held me while I cried. Or the way he had helped me work in the bakery or the way he'd gone down on me and made me come so hard…

The problem was, I'm just not the kind of person who can give her body without giving her heart. It was yet another reason I had stopped dating—all the guys on the dating apps seemed to want was a quick hook-up. I can't do that. For me, the emotional goes along with the physical. Sex ought to *mean* something—that's how I feel, anyway.

So even though I had known the big Incubus less than twenty-four hours, I still felt like my heart had been run through a meat grinder. It *hurt* and what hurt even more was knowing that I was never going to see Malik again.

CHAPTER FOURTEEN

"Uh, hi." Sarah gave me a cautious look as she came in the door of the bakery, already dressed in her baker's whites.

"Hi," I muttered, not looking up from the stainless-steel counter I was staring at.

After much debate, I had decided to open The Lost Lamb as usual —mostly because I don't believe in hiding from the consequences of your actions. Even though it was an accident, I had to take responsibility.

"So…I hear there was a lot of excitement yesterday," Sarah said tactfully as she came around the counter to join me. "How are you doing?"

"About as well as you can expect considering that I gave everyone in Hidden Hollow a magical aphrodisiac," I said tartly.

"Yeah, that was, er, strong stuff in the tarts," she murmured. "Rath brought some home for us to share and well…" She shook her head. "The sex was incredible, if that's any consolation."

"It's not," I snapped. Then I sighed. "Look, I'm sorry Sarah but I'm afraid I'll have to let you go."

"Let me go? Why?" She gave me a wide-eyed look full of shock. "I don't understand!"

I sighed again.

"It has nothing to do with you—it's just that I'm afraid I'll probably have to shut down the bakery. After all, who's going to trust me enough to eat a single thing I make after I poisoned them all yesterday?"

"You didn't *poison* anyone!" Sarah exclaimed indignantly. "It's not like you dumped a jar of rat poison in the tarts—you just got people excited to be with the ones they love!"

"Tell that to Goody Albright," I said glumly and then relayed everything that had happened the night before.

"Oh my—none of them under five hundred?" Sarah's eyes went wide. "How are they doing this morning?"

"I don't know but I'm sure Goody Albright has her hands full. I should probably go down and apologize and take responsibility in person as soon as it's breakfast time," I said morosely. "The Red Lion serves breakfast from eight to nine-thirty so if I go down there around nine, I should be able to catch most of the members of The Council of Wisdom. I hope anyway."

"Well, that should help some," Sarah acknowledged. "But I really think you're overestimating the number of people who will be upset. I mean, a lot of people will probably be happy with what happened— Rath and I had the best sex we'd had since we bonded as Heartmates last night."

"But what about all the single people who probably hooked up with strangers—or people they never met before?" I demanded. "What about people who just stopped in for a treat or dessert and didn't expect —oh my God!" I slapped a hand over my mouth.

"What? What is it?" Sarah asked, looking worried.

"Goldie! I gave her two dozen tarts to serve at the diner yesterday and I forgot to warn her! Oh my God, I should have called her last night!"

Goldie's diner stays open later than any other business in Hidden

Hollow, which meant she had probably been serving the tarts for some time after I had found out what happened the night before.

"I'll get her on the phone," Sarah was already dialing. But when she put her phone on speaker and held it out, all we heard was ringing over and over. Then finally we got a message,

"This is Goldie from Goldie's Diner. If you missed me, you know what to do—leave a message and I'll get back when I can. And if you can't wait, come on in to the diner for a slice of pie and I'll see you then. Toodles!"

There was a click and for a moment Sarah and I just stared at each other. Then I grabbed the phone and started talking.

"Goldie, this is Celia. It may be too late to tell you this, but please don't serve anyone the Golden Warbler tarts you picked up yesterday! There was a…a problem with them. Anyway, don't serve them and don't eat them!"

The phone beeped at me before I could add any more and I handed the phone back to Sarah.

"I'm really worried that she didn't answer—she should already be opening for breakfast!" I said and started pacing. "Maybe I should go check on her."

"I'll go," Sarah said at once. "You stay here. I'll be back to help start this morning's pastries in a few minutes."

I shook my head glumly.

"Why bother to make anything? Nobody's going to want to buy it."

"Yes, they will!" Sarah insisted. "Look, Celia, the people of this town *love* you. They won't hold a grudge. Just let them know that you made a mistake and you're sorry and it won't happen again. They'll understand."

"Well, I can absolutely *promise* that it won't happen again," I said glumly. The only reason it had happened in the first place was that being around Malik made me so unrelentingly hot and bothered. Now that the big Incubus was gone, I was absolutely *not* feeling even remotely horny—just sad.

Sarah left to go to the diner but she was back shortly with a worried look on her face.

"They're closed," she said. "I haven't been in town as long as you, but I don't remember Goldie's ever being closed before."

I groaned and shook my head.

"She's probably at home hating me because I poisoned her clients too."

"Will you stop with that poisoning stuff?" Sarah demanded. "I'm telling you, you didn't poison *anyone*. Now come on, let's make a batch of blueberry muffins and some cinnamon rolls."

Her brisk words got me moving and we spent the next couple of hours getting several batches of baked goods out. Even though I was sure I was going to have to throw them all away since no one would buy them, the act of baking soothed my soul, as it always had. By the time the doors opened I was braced for the first customer, an apology ready on my lips.

The first ones through the door were Hubert and his wife Zelda. The two of them are red Dwarves that live on the far end of town and both of them have reddish-gold beards. (Yes, Dwarf women almost all have beards—that's normal for them, although Zelda wore hers considerably shorter than her husband's, which was down to his belt buckle.) The two of them are regulars who love my cinnamon rolls so that was what I was expecting them to order—if they didn't curse me out instead.

"Celia, hello!" Hubert said, coming right up to the counter. He was about a head shorter than me but extremely stocky with a powerful build.

"Hi Hubert," I said warily. "Er, how can I help you?"

Hubert looked around as though someone might be watching. Leaning across the counter he murmured,

"Do you have any more of them pear tarts left to sell?"

I was surprised.

"Er, I'm afraid not." I shook my head.

"I *told* you she'd be all sold out!" Zelda exclaimed. "That kind of sex magic don't last long—especially when you're selling it cheap!"

"Are you talking about the, er, effects the pear tarts had on some people?" I asked cautiously.

"'Course I am!" Zelda exclaimed. "Those tarts got Hubie all excited for me for the first time in nigh on two years! See, he has trouble getting his pecker hard but after eating those tarts—"

"Shut up, woman!" Hubert snapped. "She don't need to know nothing about my problem! Besides, the only reason I can't get hard is *you.* You never try to make yourself sexy for me and you wear your beard so short it's hardly there at all!"

"I can't help it I can't grow a beard as long as other women," Zelda protested, putting one hand to her closely-clipped reddish gold beard. She *had* tried to make it pretty—the part growing on her chin was braided and there was a pink bow at the end of it.

"So the two of you aren't upset about how the pear tarts made you react?" I asked, just to be sure.

"No, we're just sorry you don't got no more of 'em," Zelda said sadly. "Are you sure you're not hiding just *one* more in the back?"

"I'm sorry." I held out my hands. "We sold out yesterday."

"We *do* have some fresh cinnamon rolls though," Sarah added helpfully.

"Do they got the lust spell on 'em?" Hubert asked, looking hopeful.

"I'm afraid not." I shook my head.

"Aw, too bad." He sighed deeply. "Well, give us some cinnamon rolls then. Two oughta do it."

"Regular or Creature sized?" I asked because I make a lot of extra-large pastries for the Creatures with big appetites in town.

"Better make 'em Creature sized," Hubert said. "But if you ever do make any more of them lust tarts, let us know—we want some!"

"We sure do," Zelda agreed eagerly.

"I'll, uh, keep that in mind," I said, nodding. "What happened with the pear tarts was kind of an accident. I don't know if I could duplicate it again."

In fact, I was pretty sure I couldn't. Only having Malik near me, keeping me hot and bothered, had allowed my magic to leak into the baked goods. I couldn't see myself feeling that way when I was just baking on my own or baking with Sarah.

"That's too bad. You could make a mint if you sold those on the regular," Zelda told me as she and Hubert accepted the extra-large white paper bag containing two hubcap-sized cinnamon rolls. "I know I'd certainly pay for 'em. Why, Hubie's pecker got so hard—"

"Hush, woman!" Hubert snapped. "I told you, stop talking about my pecker!"

The two of them walked out of the store, still arguing. The moment the door closed behind them, I turned to Sarah, whose eyes were dancing with suppressed amusement.

"Well, that was weird," I said.

"Not just weird—hilarious!" She burst into peals of laughter. "Oh my God, I just *can't* with those two! Who knew you were selling some kind of magical Viagra in those tarts?"

"*I* certainly didn't know," I pointed out, laughing as well. "Of course, I didn't even know I'd put a lust spell on the tarts. Not that it was a spell, exactly…"

"What *was* it anyway? I mean, how did it happen?" Sarah asked curiously. All morning she'd been keeping quite while we worked, clearly trying to respect my feelings. But now that we had laughed together, she felt free to ask.

I didn't mind—I needed someone to talk to and Sarah is a great listener. I explained about how I had inherited a Demon—Malik—from my Great Aunt and everything that had happened afterwards.

"Wow!" Her eyes were wide by the time I finished. "So your emotions leaked into your baking because of your new Incubus boyfriend?"

"He's *not* my boyfriend," I protested. "He's not anything now—he left because I yelled at him over the tarts." I sighed, feeling sad all over again. "I wish I hadn't been so hasty."

"You were upset," Sarah pointed out. "Besides, all relationships have problems. I'm sure he'd come back if you called for him. Or maybe summoned him? I don't know how to go about getting a Demon to come to you," she added apologetically.

"I don't either but it doesn't matter. He's never going to want to see me again," I said dolefully. "Right now, he's probably back in Hell's Waiting Room waiting for his next assignment. Or maybe he's already *on* his next assignment, making some other witch feel horny and desirable."

Just the thought of Malik with another woman made me green with envy and sad at the same time. I didn't even want to imagine it, so I did my best to push it out of my mind.

Luckily, I was helped by the fact that the bakery started getting busy—even more busy than usual. Some of the customers were there to complain, as I had anticipated. I apologized profusely and explained that the lusty tarts had been a magical mistake. And to my surprise, most people really did seem willing to forgive me. Maybe it was because a lot of them were magic users themselves who had gotten spells wrong in the past.

The bigger surprise, though, was the number of customers who came in asking for more of the tarts or any pastry, really, that had the "lust spell" in it.

"You don't know how rare it is to find a good aphrodisiac with no negative after effects," one plain-spoken witch who had apparently really enjoyed the effects of the tarts told me. "Most of them leave you feeling hung-over something terrible the next day! Or they make your boobs swell up to the size of balloons and start shooting nectar. Or if you're a man, your tallywhacker gets as big as a baseball bat and the cum shoots out like a fire hose!"

"Oh my," I said blankly. "I had no idea."

"It's true." She nodded. "So if you ever decide to make more of those tarts with the lust spell in them, let me know—I'd like to stock up!"

The only really negative reaction I got was, unsurprisingly, from the head of The Council of Wisdom when I went to The Red Lion to apologize.

"I want to take full responsibility and explain that none of what happened after you ate my pear tarts last night was in any way Goody Albright's fault," I said to the elder witches and warlocks who had assembled in the large dining room to have breakfast. Many of them looked out of sorts and grumpy—though there were a few who had a suspiciously satisfied glow.

"So it was *you* that made us all crazy!" A senior warlock with long gray hair and a bushy gray beard rose to speak. He was wearing a tall pointy hat and a cloak which made him look like a Lord of the Rings extra.

"Yes, sir. I'm so sorry," I said contritely.

"Grand Wizard Henkleman, please—I can vouch for Celia," Goody Albright said, stepping up. "I can promise you that she didn't do this on purpose."

But the elderly warlock was clearly not appeased.

"Young lady, this kind of thing is just *unacceptable!*" he exclaimed, shaking his long, crooked staff at me. "We members of The Council of Wisdom are too old to be staying up all night having sex parties! Why the chafing alone—"

"Now, Grand Wizard Henkleman, do we *really* want to go into details?" Goody Albright asked hastily.

From the coughing and clearing of throats in the room, it seemed no one really did. Still grumbling angrily and shaking his staff at me, the elderly warlock settled back into his seat.

"I'm so sorry," I said again. "I'll understand if you don't want to take me up on this, but I'd like to offer all of you any pastry of your choice to try and help make up for the inconvenience. I promise none of them are bespelled in any way," I added quickly.

"Celia is especially famous for her delicious cinnamon rolls and blueberry muffins," Goody Albright said, backing me up.

I shot her a look filled with gratitude—it was nice of her not to be mad at me and to try and help me out.

"That's what you said about her pear tarts—that they were famous!" Grand Wizard Henkleman groused. "And they kept us all up having carnal relations half the night!"

"Don't you listen to him, young lady!" An older female witch tugged at my sleeve. Her tiny raisin eyes, set in a nest of wrinkles, twinkled with glee. "I haven't enjoyed myself so much in two centuries," she whispered to me when I leaned down to hear her. "Don't you listen to Henkleman—he's just mad that nobody wanted to have fun with him, so he had to make do with an old knothole in the wall!" Her voice dipped even lower. "I think he might have got a splinter in his peter—you know?

"Oh, um…" I had *no* idea what to do with this information, but luckily she didn't wait for an answer.

"I'm sure your cinnamon rolls are *delicious,*" she went on, raising her voice so everyone could hear. "And I'd *love* to try one."

"Thank you," I said, smiling at her. "If you'd like to come over to The Lost Lamb, I'd be happy to give you one for free."

"You bet I'll come to your bakery!" she grinned at me. "We *all* will —won't we?" she added, speaking to the rest of the room at large.

There were a few mutters and gripes, but for the most part—and with the notable exception of Grand Wizard Henkelman who might or might not have gotten a splinter in his penis the night before from getting frisky with a knothole—the rest of The Council of Wisdom seemed to agree with her.

I gave the elder witch a grateful nod and thanked them all for their forgiveness. Then I excused myself and Goody Albright walked me to the front door.

"Well, that went better than we could have hoped for, I think," she said, beaming at me as we stepped out onto the wide front porch. "You're lucky that Goody Tandy took a liking to you—that's the witch who got everyone to promise to stop by the bakery," she added. "It was nice of you to come apologize in person."

"Of course," I said. "I couldn't let you take responsibility when it was all my fault."

"Well, not *all* your fault. I'm the one who gave you the picture of the Incubus to start with," she said apologetically. "I'm so sorry—I didn't know what a mess it would make. Where *is* that handsome devil now?" she added, looking around as though Malik might suddenly appear out of thin air.

I shrugged unhappily.

"I don't know—back in Hell's Waiting Room, I guess. I haven't seen him since I told him off yesterday."

"I bet he's not too far away," she said, patting my arm. "I can tell you have feelings for him, despite the mischief he caused."

"No, I don't!" I protested.

"Oh, really?" Goody Albright looked at me skeptically over the rim of her gold spectacles. "Are you *sure* about that?"

"Okay, I *do* have feelings for Malik—but he'll never want to see me again after the way I talked to him!" I said.

"Don't be too sure about that, dear. After all, he has ties to your bloodline and your family. That counts for a lot in the magical world," she told me. "All you need to do is call his name and I bet he'll appear instantly."

"I just don't—" I began but just then a strange looking person came up the porch steps and approached me.

"Excuse me, but are you Celia Hatch?" she asked. She was wearing a long black cloak that rustled when she walked and her face was extremely ugly with a large, beak-like nose, thin lips, and narrow orange eyes.

"Er, yes—that's me," I said.

"Good. I'm here to serve you with some legal documents," she said, pronouncing it "dawk-uments" in a voice that sounded like the cawing of a crow.

"Legal documents?" I said, feeling my stomach drop to the floor. "You mean because of the pear tarts?"

"Exactly." She nodded and spread her cloak open—I realized when she did why it had been rustling. It was made of long black feathers the length of my arm. Underneath she was wearing a black business suit and her legs, when they were revealed, were spindly and yellow. They ended in three-toed feet that looked like enormous bird's feet.

I couldn't figure out what kind of Creature the woman was—maybe a Harpy? At any rate, she clearly wasn't human. However, I was more concerned about the documents she was holding out to me than placing exactly what magical species she was.

"What are these for?" I asked, looking down at the documents which were covered in a tiny, dense script I didn't think I'd be able to read without a microscope. "Is someone upset about the, er, effects of the pear tarts?"

"Not quite—this is a suit brought against you by Mr. Goremouth," she said in her cawing voice.

"Who?" I shook my head—I didn't remember having a customer with that name.

"Mr. Guglor Goremouth—the Ogre you stole the Golden-Skinned Warbler pears from in order to make your tarts," she snapped. "He's summoning you to court at once for immediate satisfaction!"

"What? You can't just—" I began.

"Yes, we can. I'm his attorney, Counselor Heketate. Here!" And she shoved the papers at me.

Goody Albright, who was still standing beside me, suddenly gripped my arm.

"No, Celia! Don't accept—" she began but my hand was already closing on the sheaf of papers.

The moment the paperwork was in my grasp, the world around me melted away. The front porch of the Red Lion and Main Street itself were suddenly gone and I was floating in a terrifying black void.

I had no idea what as happening—all I knew was that I was scared to death.

CHAPTER FIFTEEN

For a moment there was nothing but a terrifying black void all around me. Then the world began to take shape and I found I was standing in a courtroom—but it wasn't like any courtroom in the Mortal Realm.

It was a huge, shadowy room with glowing green doors on either side—one on the left and one on the right. The judge's seat was located at least ten feet above the rest of the courtroom and there was no place to sit for either the defendant or the plaintiff. Speaking of the plaintiff, where was he?

I looked to my left and saw the enormous, smelly Ogre who had chased me down the path behind my house. It appeared like he had at least tried to dress for court. His long orange pelt had been combed into some semblance of order—though to be honest, the comb tracks in it only made it look greasier since it was very clear he hadn't washed it. He was wearing longer trousers too, though still no shoes or shirt. He did however, have a lime green tie around his thick neck. It was too long and hung down almost to his crotch.

Standing by his side was the Harpy lawyer who had served me with the magical papers that caused me to appear in the courtroom. But there was no one waiting to represent me, I saw with dismay. And where was the judge? How could we have a trial without one?

As if in answer to my question, a booming, disembodied voice rang out,

"All rise for the judge and adjudicator of this case!"

Since we were all already standing, nobody moved as one of the glowing green doors opened and in walked an elderly warlock in a long black robe.

My heart sank when I saw who it was—none other than the head of The Council of Wisdom—Grand Wizard Henkelman.

I remembered now that Goody Albright had said that he and The Council went all around the world presiding over cases in the magical court system. But what terrible luck for him to be the judge of this particular case! Why couldn't I have gotten Goody Tandy, the sweet old witch who wanted to try my cinnamon rolls instead?

I tried to think of all the court cases I used to watch on Judge Judy back when I was a kid and I was home sick from school. Could I ask the judge to recuse himself from my case on the grounds that he was already prejudiced against me since my lust-filled pear tarts had caused him to screw a knothole and get a splinter in his privates? I didn't know and I was afraid that if I made a motion like that and it was denied, Grand Wizard Henkelman would get even angrier at me.

The elderly warlock went to the base of the extremely tall podium that dominated the room and began to climb. After a few minutes of audible huffing and puffing, he arrived at last at the top and settled himself on the judge's bench. He reached into his long black judge's robe and pulled out a tiny silver gavel which he tapped lightly on the podium.

It must have been magical because instead of the soft *tink-tink-tink* I expected, a loud *BOOM! BOOM! BOOM!* rang out across the shadowy courtroom.

"Now then, this court will come to order!" Grand Wizard Henkelman shouted, as though everyone was yelling instead of just standing quietly, watching him. "Bailiff—will you please state the case and read the charges?" he added.

"This is the case of the Ogre, Guglor Goremouth, who is suing the witch, Celia Hatch, for the unlawful theft of his property," the loud, disembodied voice which had announced the judge in the first place said.

"I see. Yes, yes." Grand Wizard Henkelman nodded importantly. "Well, attorneys—let's hear the facts of the case! Councilor Heketate, you may speak first," he added, looking down at the Ogre's lawyer. "Please step forward and tell me what happened."

"Thank you, Your Honor." The Harpy stepped forward and shook out her wings with a rustle. "Here are the facts of the case. Yesterday, on the twenty-second day of September, the year of our Goddess two thousand and twenty four, this witch, Celia Hatch, trespassed on my client's property—"

"I didn't trespass!" I exclaimed.

Grand Wizard Henkelman tapped his silver gavel again, which resulted in a loud *BOOM-BOOM!* and glared down at me.

"That will be quite enough of that! You may speak when you're spoken to—not before!"

"But she's lying!" I said desperately. "I never trespassed on anyone's property—I was on a path that runs behind my house."

"Enough!" Grand Wizard Henkelman pointed one long crooked finger at me. "I already know what a troublemaker you are, witch! You'll get your turn to state your case. For now, be silent or I'll charge you with Contempt of Court!"

I wasn't sure what the penalty was for Contempt of Court in a magical court and I didn't want to find out. Unhappily, I nodded and murmured,

"Yes, Your Honor."

"Good. Now maybe we can continue. Councilor Heketate?" he said, turning back to the Harpy lawyer.

"Thank you, Your Honor," she said, fluffing her wings. "As I was saying, the witch, Celia Hatch, trespassed on my client's property and proceeded to steal dozens of valuable and magical Golden-Skinned Warbler pears which she took from the tree that grows in his yard and made into tarts which she then sold for profit. My client is asking for fair compensation for the theft."

"I see. What a heinous act!" Grand Wizard Henkelman declared, staring sternly at me. "*Especially* since we know she used those pears to make lust-filled tarts that forced unsuspecting persons into copulation with inanimate objects which resulted in great personal pain in their private areas!"

I wanted to groan—great, just great. So he *had* gotten a splinter in his sausage. And it was clear he was going to hold it against me, even though it had been an accident.

"Please, Your Honor—" I began.

"Silence!" Grand Wizard Henkelman roared. "I'm ready to rule!"

"What? But you haven't even heard my part yet!" I protested.

"All right—what have you to say for yourself, witch?" he demanded.

"What I said before—that the pears I took were on branches that hung over the path where I was walking," I said. "I never climbed over the hedge and went onto Mr. er, Goremouth's property. Also, I've been picking these pears for five years now and I've never even seen him around before—I thought the house he's apparently living in was empty and deserted!"

I was hoping my explanation would clear my name but the head of The Council of Wisdom only glared harder.

"So, you not only admit to stealing the pears this year, you admit that you've been stealing them for the past *five* years as well?" he demanded. "This is *outrageous!*"

Uh-oh—clearly I had just made things worse for myself. What could I do to save this situation? Nothing, apparently, because Grand Wizard Henkelman tapped with his gavel again—*BOOM-BOOM!*—and declared,

"I've heard enough! I'm ready to rule. Since the plaintiff has admitted to her guilt—"

"Wait!" I exclaimed desperately.

"How *dare* you interrupt me in the middle of sentencing?" Henkelman shouted.

"Because…because…" I looked around the shadowy courtroom desperately and my eyes fastened on the Harpy lawyer. "Because I don't have an attorney to speak for me!" I exclaimed, hoping against hope that this would work. "It's not fair that the Ogre—Mr. Goremouth—has a lawyer and I don't!"

"If you wanted an attorney present, you should have retained legal counsel, like Mr. Goremouth did," the judge snapped.

"How could I?" I demanded. "The first I heard of this case was when the Harpy—er, Councilor Heketate—served me the papers which immediately caused me to vanish from Hidden Hollow and appear here, in this courtroom!"

I was afraid that Grand Wizard Henkelman would simply ignore my protests but he got a thoughtful look on his face.

"Very well—since you neglected to retain your own legal council, an attorney will be provided for you," he said. "In fact, I know just the one! A Centaur who has one of the finest young legal minds in the entire magical world."

"Oh, thank goodness!" I murmured, feeling the fist of tension that had gathered in the pit of my stomach unclenching just a bit.

But the next minute, I clenched up again, even harder. Because when the green door the judge had come from opened again, it was Chester the deaf Centaur I saw coming through. Was he really a lawyer? I guessed that he must be, but I was sure he'd been retired for ages. I had once heard another customer in the bakery saying he was over three hundred years old—magic users and Creatures tend to be long-lived. Even if he was a lawyer though, how could Henkelman describe him as "one of the finest *young* legal minds in the entire magical world?"

I guess maybe everyone seems young when you're over five hundred years old yourself, I thought, remembering what Goody Albright had said about the advanced age of everyone who was on The Council of Wisdom.

"Hey, what's all this—a trial?" the Centaur demanded, squinting up at the judge.

"Councilor Chester," Grand Wizard Henkelman said importantly. "Welcome to my courtroom."

"Eh?" Chester cocked his head to one side and looked confused.

"I said, *WELCOME TO MY COURTROOM!*" Henkelman bawled.

"Oh, yes." Chester nodded vaguely. "A courtroom—so it is. I haven't been in a courtroom in donkey's years!"

"You have been called here to represent this young witch, who has stolen pears from this Ogre," Henkelman told him.

"Eh? What now? She stole hairs from him?" Chester squinted at the Ogre across from us. "Looks hairy enough to me—she must not have stolen many!"

"No, no!"

The Grand Wizard looked irritated. He tapped his silver gavel on the podium once more but this time instead of producing a loud *BOOM!* it twisted in his hand and began to grow. A moment later it had become an old-fashioned ear trumpet with a wide silver bell on one end and a mouthpiece on the other to shout into. Henkelman tapped it again and it grew until it was long enough to reach from the top of the very tall judge's bench all the way down to Chester's ear. Then he shouted loudly,

"I said, you are here to represent this witch who stole the pears of this Ogre from the pear tree in his yard!"

"Stole them did she?" Chester frowned down at me. "Well what do you want me to do about it? Sounds to me like she's guilty."

"No, no, Chester!" I said desperately. "You're supposed to be my attorney! You have to defend me!"

"Send you? Send you where?" he asked, frowning.

"No, not send—DEFEND," I bawled at him. Unfortunately he was quite tall—all Centaurs are, due to being half horse—and I couldn't get anywhere near his ear. He did seem to get the idea, however.

"Defend you? But the judge says you're guilty of stealing! I don't take guilty clients, Missy," he said.

"But I'm *NOT GUILTY!*" I shouted desperately. "The pears I picked were on branches outside the Ogre's land!"

"Got a lot of sand, does he?" Chester demanded. "Did you steal that too?"

This was hopeless! I was beginning to get horrible visions of being thrown in a magical jail to rot forever. Chester, who had always seemed nice, if a little vague, was turning out to be no help at all. In fact, I was pretty sure he was making things worse for me.

"Please, Your Honor, I need another attorney," I said, turning to look up at Grand Wizard Henkelman. "This isn't working out at all."

The judge looked incensed.

"Absolutely not! I got you the finest legal mind in all of the magical world and you have the nerve to ask for a different counselor instead? Preposterous!"

"But he can't hear me! He can't understand!" I exclaimed. "And he might have been the finest legal mind before he retired but he's three hundred years old now!"

"What is your point?" Henkelman snapped. "I will have you know, witch, that I am *six hundred* years old myself! Age does not dull one's knowledge of the Law. In fact, it rather refines it—a good legal mind ages like fine wine!"

"What sign?" Chester asked, looking around. "I don't see any sign. Does it have anything to do with the hairs and the sand?"

Henkelman looked miffed.

"Enough of this," he declared. "I'm ready to rule."

"What? But—" I began.

"Silence!" Grand Wizard Henkelman thundered, glaring down at me from the judge's bench. "One more word out of you, witch, and it's Contempt of Court!"

I didn't want that. Reluctantly, I held my tongue and waited for the sentence. What else could I do?

"I judge this witch guilty of stealing the personal property of Mr. Goremouth and declare that she must pay just recompense for her theft," Henkelman announced. "Counselor Heketate," he said to the Harpy lawyer. "What is your client asking for in terms of compensation?"

"Well, Your Honor, the Golden-Skinned Warbler pears are *extremely* rare and valuable," she said, frowning. "Some experts have judged them to be worth as much as a thousand gold apiece. And since she stole at least a hundred of them…"

My heart nearly stopped in my chest. A hundred thousand gold? I didn't have that kind of money—I would have to mortgage The Lost Lamb to pay even half such a large amount!

I couldn't keep silent anymore.

"If it's money you want, I can pay for the pears!" I exclaimed. "But a thousand apiece is crazy!"

"Silence!" Henkelman pounded on his podium again—*BOOM-BOOM-BOOM!*—(the ear trumpet had turned back into a gavel) and gave me the nastiest look imaginable. "You will pay whatever the plaintiff in this case asks for!" he shouted at me.

Suddenly Goremouth the Ogre, who had been silent up until now, spoke up in his low, grating voice.

"Don't you worry, sweety-sweet—I don't want money, only meat."

I frowned at him.

"What are you talking about? What meat?"

Instead of answering me, the Ogre bent down and murmured in his attorney's ear. I watched with apprehension, wondering what he was saying. I was also wondering how in the world the Harpy lawyer could stand to be that close to him when he was so smelly.

After a moment he straightened and his lawyer looked up at the judge.

"Excuse me, Your Honor, but my client has explained what form of compensation he desires."

Henkelman nodded importantly.

"Please state it for the record, Counselor."

"Very well, since the witch stole a rare and valuable food commodity from my client, he wishes to be recompensed in kind. To wit, he wants food in return."

"I see. That sounds reasonable. What kind of food does he desire?" Henkelman asked.

"I want witch meat—good and sweet!" Goremouth grated.

"Witch meat? What does *that* mean?" I demanded. The tight fist in my midsection was getting even tighter but I told myself not to panic. Surely he didn't mean what I thought he meant.

The Harpy lawyer didn't answer me—instead, she kept talking to the judge.

"Since the witch stole and ate my client's valuable magical pears, we feel that it would be just compensation for my client, Mr. Goremouth, to be allowed to eat the witch who stole from him," she said.

"Hmm…" Henkelman frowned. "Is there legal precedent you can site for such a ruling, Counselor?"

"Certainly, Your Honor. In the case of Hansel and Gretel Vs. Broomhilda the witch. The accused children ate large holes in her valuable house, which was made of candy. When she sued for compensation, Judge Ornkill awarded her the right to eat the children in return. Unfortunately, they pushed her into her own oven and escaped, but the ruling still stands," she replied.

My body felt cold all over.

"What…what are you talking about?" I asked through numb lips. "You can't be seriously thinking about letting the Ogre *eat me?*"

"Silence young lady!" Henkelman shouted at me. "That is *exactly* what I propose to do. It seems to me that eating you is a very fair compensation for the loss of Mr. Goremouth's valuable pears!"

"But I'll *die!*" I protested. "You can't have me executed just for taking some pears!" I turned to Chester who was watching the proceedings with a vague look on his horsy face. "Chester, do something—*say something*. He's about to eat me!"

"Seat you?" the Centaur asked, frowning. "Where? I don't see any chairs in here."

Realizing there was no help coming from that direction, I turned back to the judge.

"Your Honor, this is a gross miscarriage of justice!" I exclaimed. Then I had a sudden inspiration. "What will the rest of The Council of Wisdom think when they find out you allowed me to be killed over a basketful of pears?" I demanded.

At last something I said seemed to get through to the obstinate old judge.

"Well..." He coughed and cleared his throat. "Very well—I will modify my judgment somewhat," he said.

Oh, thank God! I nearly sagged in relief. But it was short-lived.

"I will not order you to submit to being eaten without a struggle," Henkelman said. "I will allow you to fight the Ogre for your life. If you can best him, he cannot eat you."

"What?" I squeaked. "But...but he's eleven feet tall! And he's a Creature!"

"Very well—you may use your magic to fight him as well as your physical strength," Henkelman said, as though he was doing me a great favor.

"I'm a Kitchen Witch!" I protested. "My magic is only good for baking—not fighting!"

"Well, it's plenty good enough for tricking people into copulating with knotholes, isn't it?" he snapped.

"That was an accident, Your Honor!" I protested. "How could I know that you would stick your dick in a hole in the wall and get a splinter?"

I realized that I shouldn't have said it as soon as the words were out of my mouth because Henkelman's face turned positively puce with rage and he pointed at me with his gavel.

"My judgment is final! You may fight the Ogre to try and preserve your own life but if he beats you, he is fully entitled to eat you in whatever way he chooses."

"Ah, so sweet the meat!" Goremouth snarled, a large grin spreading on his dirty face to show his curving, dagger-like teeth. "Come on, girly —put up a fight! Makes your meat taste extra right!"

He began coming towards me and I shrank back away from him. I got ready to fight for my life—maybe I could kick him in the balls— when Chester suddenly spoke up again.

"A champion!" he said loudly.

"A what?" I looked up at the old Centaur uncertainly.

The vagueness had cleared from Chester's face and he seemed to have finally grasped the situation.

"I said a champion!" he exclaimed. "When the match is unfair, the accused has a right to call a champion to fight for them!"

"You heard him!" I looked up at Grand Wizard Henkelman with desperate hope. "This match is extremely unfair! I should have the right to call a champion to defend me!"

The grumpy wizard looked like he wanted to disagree but apparently Chester had hit on some kind of legal precedent in the magical courts because at last he nodded.

"Oh, very well. Call for a Champion," he said. "But be quick about it! This case has taken far too long already."

I patted my pockets, but to my horror, I found I didn't have my phone. And even if I did, who could I call? Maybe Sarah could convince Rath to fight for me—the big Orc could probably take on the Ogre. But without a phone, how could I ask for help?

"I don't have my phone with me," I said to Grand Wizard Henkelman.

He yawned widely.

"That's too bad. This court does not supply communication devices —especially to convicted criminals!"

"Chester," I said, turning to the Centaur. "I need a phone! A PHONE!"

But the vague look was back on his face again.

"A lone? Sorry but I don't lone money to clients," he said, stamping his back hoof. "Bad policy to start that, don't you know!"

Well, he probably didn't have a phone anyway. Where would he keep it? After all, it wasn't like Centaurs could wear trousers, so they didn't have any pockets. Desperately I thought of anything else I could do.

Then I remembered something Goody Albright had said to me.

"All you need to do is call his name and I bet he'll appear instantly," she'd said, when talking to me about Malik.

I had no idea if she was right or not but there was nothing left to try.

Lifting my voice, I shouted as loudly as I could,

"Malik! *Malik!*"

Nothing happened and no one came, but I wasn't giving up. Maybe he had to be summoned instead of just called.

"Malik, Incubus of Hell, I, Celia Hatch call on you now to come and fight for me!" I shouted.

Still nothing. I tried again.

"By the bloodline of my ancestress, Hester Hatch, I bid you to appear, Malik! Come to me *NOW!*" I bawled so loudly that my voice echoed through the entire cavernous room.

But still, no one came. Malik didn't appear to save me like he had on the path behind my house. There was no sign of his muscular body or charming smile. There was just nothing…I was all alone with no one to stop the Ogre from eating me.

I was about to call again when Henkelman banged his gavel once more.

"That is *enough*. You've had three calls and your champion has not arrived. I order you to give yourself over to the party you injured so grievously for compensation," he commanded importantly.

"Like Hell, I will!" I muttered. *I* was the one who was going to be grievously injured if Goremouth caught me! As the Ogre reached for me again, I dodged away and ran to the far corner of the big room.

This didn't seem to bother Goremouth a bit. In fact, he was grinning from ear to ear as he came for me, his long hairy arms outstretched to catch me.

"Come now girly, time to eat. You're going to be old Goremouth's treat," he grated, grinning that horrible toothy grin.

If only he wasn't so *big*, I thought desperately! He wasn't very fast but even one of his strides was like three of mine. How could I possibly get away?

I caught a flash of green from the corner of my eye. The doors!

I skittered away from the Ogre's grasp at the last minute, aiming for the closest glowing green door. But when I got to it, the handle wouldn't turn. It just twisted back and forth in my sweaty palm and no matter how much I tugged, the door wouldn't open. Even worse, Goremouth was only a few feet behind me!

Heart pounding with fear, I ran to the other door on the other side of the courtroom. To my surprise, the Ogre didn't try to stop me this time. He just stood there grinning that evil, hungry grin.

"Go on girly, run—be free. We shall see what we shall see," he growled.

Never taking my eyes from him, I twisted the knob. It nearly slipped in my sweaty palm but then—oh, thank God!—I felt it turn.

With a gasp, I shoved the door open and—not even looking where I was going—dashed through it and slammed it shut behind me.

Safe—I was safe!

Or so I thought.

CHAPTER SIXTEEN

The green door disappeared as soon as I was through it and I found myself in a strange, cavernous room. It was dimly lit and at first, I was afraid that I was back in the awful courtroom again. But after looking around, I realized that I was wrong. The room was big and dim, just like the courtroom had been, but it was definitely different.

For one thing, instead of an empty space with nothing but the tall judge's bench, this room was crowded with furniture. There was an enormous wooden table and two huge chairs sitting in the center of the room. Also, the walls were lined with extremely high counters that came up past my head. In one corner was a massive iron stove—the kind you see when you go visit one of those museums that show how people lived in the past before electricity.

Someone had built a fire in the stove and there was an enormous cook-pot, as big as a bathtub, sitting on its red-hot surface. It was filled with water which was just beginning to boil. Sitting on the counter beside the stove was what looked like a cutting board the size of a child's snow sled. On it was a knife as big as a machete. The curving blade looked wickedly sharp.

"A kitchen," I whispered, looking around me. "I'm in a giant's kitchen. How did I get here? And where *is* here anyway?"

There was a kitchen window but it was much too high for me to look out of. Luckily, one of the wooden chairs was in a good position. Using the rungs of the chair, I hoisted myself up and stood on its seat. I peered out of the window, looking for any kind of landmark that might tell me where I was.

The scene outside was idyllic, if a little wild. There was an overgrown lawn which led up to a tall evergreen hedge that seemed to run the entire length of the property. Growing right up against the hedge was a tree whose branches seemed to droop over to the other side…wait a minute.

My heart seemed to stop in my chest. I knew where I was now. That tree and that hedge were familiar. It was the same hedge I walked beside every day when I took the path behind my house. And the tree was the Golden-Skinned Warbler pear tree—in fact, it still had fruit on it! Could it be that this side of the tree kept its fruit even though I had picked all the pears from the other side? Was it some kind of magical boundary thing?

But I didn't have long to think about that because it was becoming clear where I was. I was inside the haunted mansion—inside Goremouth's house! I wasn't safe at all—I had walked right into my enemy's lair.

"Oh my God!" I whispered, feeling sick.

Suddenly the giant kitchen seemed to give off a much more ominous vibe. The boiling water in the bathtub-sized pot…the enormous cutting board…the machete-sized knife—were they all meant for me?

They must be and here I was standing around like an idiot instead of trying to get out! Scrambling down off the chair so fast I nearly fell in my haste, I hurried to the far side of the kitchen to see if I could get out the back door.

But when I reached it, my heart dropped. The knob was so high off the ground I couldn't reach it!

I jumped up, trying to catch hold of it—it was as big as a volleyball but I thought if I could just get my hands on either side of it and twist…

And then a low, grating voice spoke behind me.

"Forget it, girly—it's too late. Now you'll go on Goremouth's plate."

Turning, I saw the Ogre standing there with a hungry, leering grin on his ugly face.

Trapped—I was trapped again and this time there was no way out!

CHAPTER SEVENTEEN

"Stay away from me—leave me alone!" I backed slowly away, only to find that I was standing in a corner. I wanted to dodge away—maybe run to a different part of the house—but the Ogre was suddenly there, right in front of me. Moving more quickly than I would have believed possible, he reached out and grabbed me by my upper arm.

"Now I have you, girly-mine. Almost time to wine and dine," he snarled, grinning at me.

"No! Let me go!" I threw myself backwards, doing my best to get away from the stinking monster. I nearly dislocated my shoulder but it was all in vain, Goremouth only tightened his grip on my arm and dragged me closer.

He was still wearing his court clothes—dirty brown trousers and the long green necktie which looked ridiculous around his thick neck. His scent was all around me—unwashed flesh and rotten garbage—it made me want to puke!

"Come with me and we will see, how nice and fresh your tasty flesh," he grated and began dragging me towards the cutting board and the stove.

"No! *No!*" I shrieked. "Help! Help me!"

But there was no one there to help—just me all alone in a monster's kitchen about to become the Ogre's supper. Desperately, I looked for anything at all I could do to stop him—anything to help me get the upper hand.

My eyes fell again on his dangling, lime-green necktie. Leaning forward on impulse, I grabbed it with my free hand and yanked hard to one side.

As I had hoped, this tightened the loop of the tie around Goremouth's thick neck. I pulled as hard as I could and was rewarded with a choking sound. The Ogre's face turned red and he grabbed for the tie.

"Nasty bitch, you little witch!" he wheezed.

For a moment I thought I really had him—and I might have if I could have pulled with both hands. Unfortunately, I wasn't strong enough to actually strangle him one-handed. The minute he grabbed for the tie, he was able to pull it out of my grip. Then he loosened it with his free hand and glared down at me.

"That's not nice—you go on ice!" he declared. "But first a chop to make you hop!"

Reaching for me with both hands, he swung me with dizzying speed up to the chopping board that was sitting on the counter.

He was just reaching for the machete-sized knife when a deep, familiar voice spoke behind him.

"How many times do I have to tell you to leave my woman alone?"

"What?" Goremouth spun around, taking both hands off me in his haste to see who was in his kitchen. As he moved out of the way, I saw a familiar face and felt a wave of relief.

Malik! He was here—he had finally come to save me!

CHAPTER EIGHTEEN

M alik had gotten big and scary again, but the Ogre was still bigger.

"You fucker," the Incubus growled and I saw the Hellfire burning in his black eyes as he glared at Goremouth. "I told you if you ever touched her again you were going to pay! Now you *die.*"

He lunged for the Ogre but spun away at the last minute just as Goremouth was reaching out long arms to grapple. Instead of closing with his much larger adversary, the Incubus whipped his tail around.

In a moment of slow-motion clarity, I saw that the pointed triangular tip at the end of the tail had grown incredibly long and sharp —almost like a dagger. And was that a droplet of bright green poison I saw on the end of it?

Then the moment was over and I saw the tip of Malik's tail plunge into one of the Ogre's beady little eyes.

"Arrrgh!" Goremouth howled. Clapping one meaty hand over his hurt eye, he staggered backwards. His big body hit the countertop I was on, nearly knocking me over but somehow I kept my balance. And I saw an opportunity.

I've never been much of a fighter—I'd rather stay inside and bake cookies than stand up to a bully any day. But this was a matter of life and death and they say when you get into that situation it's a fight or flight scenario.

I chose to fight.

Picking up the machete-sized butcher knife, I swung it as hard as I could at the Ogre's thick neck. Probably it would have worked better if I had sliced with the knife instead of chopping like it was an ax, but the wound I made was still pretty deep. A river of black, ichorous blood began to ooze out to make his greasy orange fur even dirtier.

"No! Hurts!" the Ogre screamed, grabbing for his neck with the hand that wasn't clutching at his eye. Apparently being in pain made him forget to rhyme—how interesting.

I drew back and hacked at him from behind again. Goremouth turned to face me, grabbing blindly with the hand that had been holding his eye. I noticed that it was nothing but a slit now, oozing black blood just like his wounded neck.

"I'll get you, bitch!" he grated, his voice gravelly with pain.

I was trying to slide out of the way and hack at his reaching hand with the knife at the same time when Malik took a sudden leap and landed on the Ogre's back. He gripped the green necktie and pulled —hard.

The big Incubus was strong enough to do what I hadn't been able to. Goremouth's ugly face went purple almost at once as the lime green tie cut off his air. He tried to roar but it came out as a breathless wheeze and then Malik's tail whipped around and stung him again, in the other eye.

The Ogre howled in agony but it came out as a gasp. Completely blind now, he blundered around the kitchen, knocking over the chairs and running into the table. Malik clung to his back like a rider determined not to be bucked off an angry bull. Gripping the necktie, he somehow steered the Ogre back to the stove and the pot of water, which was now at a rolling boil.

"Celia, get out of the way!" he shouted at me.

I barely had time to hop down from the kitchen counter—the machete-knife still in my hand—before Malik grabbed the Ogre's head and forced it forward and down, straight into the pot of boiling water.

Goremouth went crazy! His long ape-like arms started flailing and his big body was fishtailing helplessly. Somehow Malik kept him in place with his head in the pot. I noticed his tail whipping out and stabbing down, stinging again and again with vicious speed as he incapacitated the Ogre with his venom.

At last Goremouth stopped struggling and the big body slumped forward over the stove. His fury pelt came in contact with the red-hot surface and his greasy pelt began to burn, which only added to the nauseating scent that permeated the kitchen.

"There, you fucker!" Malik stung him one last time—a vicious stab to the back of his thick neck. Then he jumped lightly away from the Ogre's corpse and came to find me.

Somehow I had ended up under the enormous table and that's where I was huddling when Malik bent down to look at me.

"Celia, are you all right, baby?" He was breathing hard, as though killing the Ogre had been an effort, but his hair still looked ridiculously perfect. And his eyes—his eyes were full of emotion. "There you are—come here. I need to hold you," he said.

And then he was pulling me out from under the table and wrapping me in his arms.

"Oh, Malik!" I moaned into the side of his neck, as tears of shock filled my eyes. "Oh, I was so sure he was going to k-kill me and eat m-me!"

"I'm so sorry, baby—I got here as soon as I could," he swore. "I heard you calling me but I couldn't reach you fast enough. I was so afraid I would be too late!"

He crushed me to him and buried his face in my hair. To my surprise, I thought I felt a few teardrops against my neck. Was the big Incubus crying? Over me?

"You're here now," I whispered. "That...that's what matters."

"Yes, baby—I'm here now. And I'm never letting you go again!"

I wanted to be held in his arms forever, but at that point my nose detected something more than hair burning. I pulled away from Malik and noticed with horror that Goremouth's body, which was still draped over the burning hot stove, was going up in flames.

"Come on—let's get out of here." Malik took me by the hand and headed for the kitchen door. Luckily he was much taller than me and opened it easily. The two of us rushed out of the haunted mansion just as the flames began to spread.

"The house—it's burning down!" I panted as tongues of flame began to lick around the doorframe. The fire was spreading with surprising rapidity considering it had only just started a minute ago.

"Let it," Malik said grimly. "That's an evil place—a lot of death and pain have happened there. Fire is a cleansing agent."

He put an arm around me and led me back to the pear tree. The two of us stood among the fragrant branches catching our breath as we watched the haunted mansion burn. It went up fast—almost like the whole place had been sprayed down with gasoline. Before we knew it, there was a raging bonfire where the Ogre's house had been and soon it would be just an enormous pile of ashes.

Once he was sure the fire wasn't going to spread, Malik turned to me.

"All right, it should be safe to get out of here now," he murmured. "Do you want to go home?"

"More than *anything*," I said fervently. I had never wanted to be safe inside the walls of the Victorian mansion my Great Aunt had left me more than I did now. "I just want to feel *safe*," I told him.

A ghost of his old charming grin came back.

"I think we can manage that."

Putting both big hands around my waist, he lifted me easily over the hedge. Then he jumped over it himself with demonic grace and landed lightly beside me.

"Come on, baby," he murmured. "Let's get out of here."

CHAPTER NINETEEN

W hen we got home, Malik insisted on taking care of me. I had complained of the awful smells at Goremouth's house—both of the Ogre himself and then the burning hair. He drew a warm bath in the old-fashioned claw-foot tub and scented the water with something sweet and light. He even undressed me and put me into it. Then he insisted on washing my hair and scrubbing me all over, as though I was a child.

"I'm not a kid, you know," I told him. "I can wash myself."

"But I don't want you to. Please, baby, I almost lost you—just let me take care of you," he begged softly.

Well, who can resist that kind of talk? I sighed and relaxed against the side of the tub as he gave me a soothing scalp massage. As his fingers caressed my scalp and washed my hair, his tail was busy with other things. It was holding a soapy sponge and washing me, almost as though it had a mind of its own. When it started washing my chest, I reached for it and held the whip-like end in my hand.

"You can certainly do a lot with this," I murmured as the tail curled around my fingers affectionately. "I can't believe you used it to kill that..." I trailed off—I didn't want to think about the awful scene in the haunted mansion—it was still too fresh, too terrible.

Of course, since he was touching me, Malik knew what was going through my head.

"Don't think about it, baby," he urged gently. "Just try and relax. Here...maybe I can give you something to take your mind off it."

The tail slipped out of my hand and curled around my right breast instead. I moaned in surprised pleasure as it gave my tight nipple a swift, painless sting.

"Oh!" I exclaimed as the nipple started to swell with pleasure and got immediately more sensitive.

Before I could say anything more, his tail slid across my chest and stung my left nipple as well.

"Mmm, do you like that?" Malik murmured, still washing my hair. "Does it feel good when I sting your beautiful nipples?"

"It...it does," I confessed. The warm water lapping against my tender peaks felt like someone licking me. It was sending sparks of pleasure through my whole body and most definitely taking my mind off the harrowing scene I'd just been through.

"Do you think you can let me sting your pussy too?" Malik murmured. "Can you be a good girl and spread your legs for me?"

I didn't answer with words. Moaning softly, I spread my thighs and watched as the long, whip-like tail slid slowly down my body. It found my pussy, just above the water, and began caressing my outer lips.

"Hmm, I think I need a little help here," Malik told me. "Can you reach down and spread yourself open for me, baby? Spread your pussy so I can sting your clit?"

I could feel my cheeks getting hot with a blush, but I couldn't deny him. Reaching between my legs, I carefully spread the outer lips of my pussy, baring myself for the big Incubus completely.

"Good girl," Malik rumbled again. "Such a good girl to spread your pussy for me, Celia."

It didn't take long for his tail to dip inside my inner folds and start teasing my clit, but to my surprise, he didn't sting me right away. Instead he seemed to enjoy circling my tight little button with the tip of his tail, sending sparks of pleasure through my entire body.

"What...what are you waiting for?" I panted. "Oh God, Malik—I'm so close!"

"I know you are and I promise I'm going to make you come in just a minute," he told me. "But before I sting your clit, I want to sting the inside of your pussy."

"Inside me?" I tilted my head up to look at him uncertainly. "Why there?"

"Because it will help you open to take me." He stroked my hair and looked down at me, a serious look in his eyes. "I didn't just come back to save you, Celia—I came back to fulfill your deepest fantasy too. In order to do that, I need you to be able to take my cock in your tight little pussy."

I felt my heart sink a little. So he wasn't here to stay—he was just going to give me mind-blowing sex and then leave. But if a beautiful memory was all I could have, then I would take it, I decided. I wasn't going to be sad or upset—I was just going to go with the flow and let him do what he wanted with me.

"All right," I said at last, letting my thighs drift further apart. "Go ahead, Malik—sting me."

His eyes went half-lidded and he bent down to give me a sweet, upside down kiss before straightening up again.

"Mmm, you're such a good girl, Celia," he told me. "Opening your pussy to let me sting you. Just relax and let me make you feel good."

As he spoke, the end of his tail slipped deep inside me and, after a moment, I felt him find the end of my channel.

"When are you going to—ohhhh!" I moaned, because it was like he had somehow found a second clit inside me and was stroking it teasingly.

I'd read many times about "G-spot orgasms" but I had always believed they were a myth. Malik proved they were for real as he continued to tease me with his tail. The pleasure was deep, like an earthquake inside me. My back arched helplessly and if Malik hadn't been holding my head as he washed my hair, I might have gone under the warm water of the bath.

"Oh…oh my God! Malik!" I moaned as his tail swelled inside me for a moment before slipping out.

"Easy, baby," he murmured, looking down at me. "Just relax."

That was easier said than done when I was still feeling the aftershocks of the deep orgasm he'd given me. Also, even though I had just come, I wanted *more*. I wanted him inside me—not just his tail but his cock, which I had yet to become acquainted with.

"I'm going to sting your clit now," Malik told me. "Not to make you come again—not yet. Just to make you more sensitive to pleasure."

As he spoke, the pointed end of his tail found my button again and I felt a slow wave of pleasure rolling through me as my clit swelled with need and desire.

"*Ohhhh*," I moaned. "Malik, I don't know if I can take much more of this! Please, I need you—need you in me!"

"You'll have me in you in just a minute, baby," he promised, his eyes half-lidded with lust. "Let me just rinse your hair and get you all dried off…"

He did as he said, washing the shampoo out of my hair and then lifting me out of the tub to dry me with a towel. I protested that I could dry myself, but he only shook his head.

"No, baby—I'm taking care of you, remember? Tonight is all about you and your pleasure," he murmured. Then he lifted me and carried me to the bed.

"Now just relax," he ordered as he laid me down on it so that my lower legs hung down over the side.

"What are you doing?" I asked as he knelt on the ground between my thighs.

"What does it look like? I'm going to taste my good girl," Malik growled, looking up to give me a hungry look.

"Please be careful!" I begged. Since he had stung me, I was feeling extremely sensitive between my legs.

"Of course, baby." Leaning forward, he placed a gentle kiss on my pussy mound. "I know you're feeling tender inside. You know I'll never hurt you."

Until you leave me, I thought but didn't say aloud. I pushed the thought out of my head almost as soon as I had it and concentrated on what Malik was doing.

"I trust you," I told him, letting my thighs drift wider apart. "Go ahead, Malik—you can taste me."

"*Mmm,* love to hear you talk like that," he growled hungrily. Then he leaned forward again and spread my outer pussy lips with his thumbs.

I bit my lip as I looked down my body and saw how swollen and needy my clit was. Clearly his pleasure venom was having an effect on me.

"I'm just going to kiss you at first," Malik murmured, looking up at me. "Just a sweet kiss on your hot little clit."

"All…all right," I panted. Being naked on the bed with him between my legs and considering all the times he'd stung me, I was feeling incredibly sensitive all over. So when he leaned down and placed a hot, open-mouthed kiss that encompassed my entire clit, I bucked my hips and moaned involuntarily—I couldn't help it.

Malik didn't lose his spot—he kept his mouth on me and then he began stroking my aching button with his hot tongue. And now I fully began to understand everything his pleasure venom could do for me. Because every soft stroke of his tongue became another orgasm—not a deep one like the one I'd had when he stung me inside my pussy or a fierce one like the last time he had gone down on me. These were feathery rushes of pleasure that flitted through my body like pulses of light which lingered, leaving a glow of happiness behind.

"Oh…*Oh!* I moaned, grabbing for his horns. "Oh God, Malik— yes…*please!*"

I heard him growl in hungry approval and then he deepened the kiss, swirling his tongue around and around my incredibly sensitive clit and making me come even harder.

He took his time pleasing me, making me come over and over, and by the time he was done, I wasn't sure I could take much more. But I still felt empty inside and I wanted him desperately. No, not wanted—I *needed* him.

"Malik..." I tugged at his horns and he looked up, his mouth shiny with my juices.

"All right, baby. I know you need to be filled," he rumbled. Climbing up on the bed with me, he settled himself in the middle with his head propped on several pillows. Then he reached for me. "Here, let's get you in the right position."

He started to pull me up on top of him, but I resisted.

"No—I want to see what I'm getting."

I opened his jeans and pulled out the biggest cock I'd ever seen in my life. Seriously it would put any porn star to shame. My eyes went wide as I stared at it. The long, thick rod of flesh was dark red. It pulsed in my hand and like the rest of his body, it was hotter than a normal human body temperature.

"Oh my God—I don't think that's going to fit!" I breathed.

"Yes, it will." He gave me a lazy smile. "That's why I stung you inside, baby. It's going to help you open up to take me. Come on now, let me show you."

He pulled me up so I was straddling him and this time I let him. I looked down between my legs where the broad, plum-shaped head of his cock was nudging my outer pussy lips.

"Are you sure about this?" I asked Malik.

He reached up to stroke my cheek.

"Of course, baby. I would never hurt you. Now can you be a good girl and come down on me so I can feel your tight little pussy wrapped around my cock?"

"I think so. I'll *try*," I said doubtfully. I still wasn't at all confident that he would be able to get that monster of a cock inside me. Seriously, it was twice as thick as my biggest toy.

But when the broad, blunt head of his cock nudged inside the mouth of my pussy, I didn't feel any pain—not even a twinge. As he pushed deeper, I could feel my inner walls stretching to take him, but again there was no pain—just a delicious sense of being opened.

"*Mmm*, look at you taking my cock so deep," Malik growled. "Look at your tight little pussy opening up for me. Good girl, Celia—take it *all.*"

I was certainly doing my best to obey. I moaned softly as I sank down on his huge shaft, feeling him filling me completely. I had never felt so open before but it was the most *amazing* feeling—the feeling of being filled by the man I loved.

Finally, I felt him bottom out inside me as I took him all the way inside. He was hot and hard inside me and when I shifted to try and get more comfortable with his huge girth stretching me out, my enlarged clit rubbed against his pelvis, sending another mini-orgasm through me.

"Oh, Malik!" I moaned helplessly as my inner walls massaged the massive cock inside me, almost as though I was begging him to fuck me and come in me.

"That's right—squeeze me with your tight little pussy!" Malik gripped my hips with his big hands and looked up at me. "Damn, you're beautiful, baby. Love to watch you sitting there and know that my cock is so deep in your tight little pussy!"

"I love it too," I panted. "But I want more—I want to feel you moving inside me."

"You want your fantasy, don't you?" Malik murmured, giving me a half-lidded smile. "All right, baby. Let me give it to you."

And then he gripped my hips harder and began to thrust.

I threw back my head and moaned as I felt him pull almost all the way out of me and then push back in. I loved that I was naked and riding him, my breasts bouncing with every deep thrust of his thick cock inside me. I loved that every time I looked down at him, he was looking back at me, his half-lidded eyes burning with lust.

And then, just as I was thinking I only needed a little more stimulation to come again, his tail came into play. First it wound around me and tugged at each of my tender nipples in turn, making me gasp and writhe with pleasure. Then it slipped down between my thighs and began teasing my clit, stroking the swollen little button over and over as Malik continued to thrust deeply into me.

Suddenly, I was right on the edge.

"Oh…oh my God!" I moaned as I felt my inner walls begin to tighten. "Oh Malik, I'm going to…going to come."

"Not far behind you, baby." His deep voice sounded strained. "Tell me, do you want me to pull out?"

I had a momentary thought—could I possibly get pregnant? But if I did, at least I'd have something to remember him by when he left and went back to Hell's Waiting Room.

"No, don't!" I moaned and to emphasize my point, I sank down lower, taking him as deep inside me as I could. "Come…come inside me!" I panted. "Fill me with your cum, Malik—I want to feel you shooting in me!"

"Damn, baby—I can't resist you when you talk like that!" he groaned. And then I felt something hot and wet spurting inside me and I knew he was giving me exactly what I wanted—filling me with his cream.

At the same time he was spurting inside me, his tail stung me on the clit again. I gasped and reached out, looking for something to hold on to as the massive wave of pleasure washed over me. Malik let go of my hips and his hands found mine.

We interlaced our fingers and, as the pleasure raced through both of us, I wished with all my heart that this never had to end. Not just the sex—though it was phenomenal. But *all* of it. I wished that we could have a life together, living in my Great Aunt's house and working in the bakery together. We might have a baby or we might just get a pet—I was long overdue to find a familiar. But whatever we did, we would do together. We would have each other to hold and comfort on the chilly Autumn nights and we would be together forever…that was my fantasy, that was my wish.

In that moment, as those thoughts formed fully in my mind, I felt something happen. It was almost as though a shining, golden cord was wrapping around my heart. But only one end of it. The other end was wrapping around Malik's heart—it was tying us together with an unbreakable energy.

"Oh!" I gasped. "What…what's happening to me?"

"To *us,*" Malik corrected me. "And the answer is, your deepest fantasy is being fulfilled."

"My deepest fantasy?" I asked, frowning. "What do you mean?"

"I mean this—*us.*" Malik smiled up at me. "Your deepest fantasy wasn't just for sex—you wanted a Heartmate. Someone to love you forever and to stay by your side."

I looked down at him, uncomprehending.

"I don't understand. Does that mean that you're…"

"I'm your Heartmate, baby. And you're mine." He let go of my hands and pulled me down so that my head was resting on his broad chest. "And I'm never letting you go."

I snuggled against his chest, breathing in his smoke and spice scent and feeling a new warmth and joy flooding through me. Malik wasn't going to go back to Hell's Waiting Room—he was going to stay right here with me. We could have the life that I'd been dreaming of and I would never have another lonely night.

And all because not long ago, I had started…Dreaming of the Demon.

EPILOGUE

"Well, don't you look like the cat that got the cream." Goldie gave me a grin as she sauntered into my shop. "You're practically glowing!"

"I'm happy," I admitted. "But I've been so worried about you! Sarah told me that the diner was closed all day yesterday and nobody knew where you had gone."

Sarah, bless her, had manned the bakery all day while I was on trial in the magical court and then later while Malik was saving me from the Ogre and then he and I were becoming Heartmates.

After all that, I had eventually thought to call her and explain why I had left the bakery and never returned. She'd been relieved that I was all right and let me know that even more people had come in asking for more of the magical "Horny pear tarts" as the customers had begun calling them.

It made me happy to know that people wanted more of the tarts because now I had a way to make them. With Malik's help, I could infuse any of my baked goods with the spirit of lust if I wanted to and I was already thinking that it might be a very lucrative side business.

But now I was back at The Lost Lamb and glad to see my friend was okay as well.

"Seriously, where have you been?" I asked Goldie. "And did you ever get the message about the tarts?"

"Oh well, I had a little *business* to attend to. And yes, I got the message—only it was too late. I had already eaten two of them myself."

"Oh, no!" I put a hand to the side of my face. "Goldie, I am *so sorry!*"

"You should be!" She wagged a finger at me, only half joking. "Do you know that I had locked up early because I wanted to take a walk? When the lust spell or whatever it was hit me, I was nowhere near home!"

"Oh my God—so what did you do?" I asked blankly.

"Well, there was this hunting lodge in the woods. I knocked but there was no one home. The door was open though." She shrugged. "So I went in."

"You went into a strange house?" I asked.

"Uh-huh, but I was getting desperate! Being overcome by lust in the middle of the forest at night isn't safe—the scent draws the wrong kind of Creatures. Luckily there were some beds upstairs so I was able to get comfortable and, er, take care of business."

"Really?" I still couldn't believe it, but she nodded coolly, as though breaking into a strange house to masturbate was no big deal.

"I stayed there in the cottage until the tarts wore off and then I was finally able to go home," she added.

"And nobody ever came home and caught you?" I asked.

"Nope." She shook her head. "I was really lucky. How can you explain that kind of thing if someone walks in on you? 'Oh sorry, I just broke into your house to touch myself because I didn't want to take my underwear off in the forest?'"

I couldn't help laughing at her words.

"Goldie, you're too much! Do you even know who lives there?"

She shook her head.

"Nope. But there were several beds and the place looked like it could use a woman's touch. It's probably owned by a couple of guys who just use it when they want to hunt."

"Well, I'm sorry again that you wound up in that situation because of my tarts," I apologized.

"Don't be." Goldie grinned and then sighed. "It was honestly the best sex I've had in ages—too bad it was all by myself."

"You should have taken a walk through town instead of the forest and tried to find a friendly Minotaur or Kraken," I said. "Almost everyone in Hidden Hollow ate one of my 'horny pear tarts' I'm sure you could have found a willing partner."

"Yeah, I wish I would have." Goldie shook her head. "Guess I'm just going to be single for life."

"No, you're not. If I can find someone, anyone can," I told her.

Her eyebrows shot up.

"You found someone? You mean it?"

"Yes—the Incubus that came out of the picture my Great Aunt left me. His name is Malik and it turns out we're Heartmates." I beamed at her. "It was my deepest fantasy to have someone to love forever and he fulfilled it."

"Aww, honey! I'm so happy for you." Goldie stood on tiptoes and reached across the counter to hug me. I hugged her back and smiled as we parted.

"Thank you. But like I said, don't give up—I'm sure there's someone out there for you."

She sighed again.

"From your lips to the Goddess's ear. This Goldie just wants to find her bears—or bear—or whatever. Just somebody who looks cute in an apron and will help at the diner during the day and screw my brains out at night."

I raised my eyebrows.

"*While* he's wearing an apron?"

"Sure—that sounds like fun." She gave me a naughty smile. "Okay, well I'd better get back to the diner but first I need a dozen cinnamon rolls and some blueberry muffins."

I got her order ready and wished her a good day. But as she left the bakery, I couldn't help wondering if Goldie might find what she was looking for next. I certainly hoped so for her sake and I felt confident that someday soon it would happen.

Because in Hidden Hollow, anything is possible.

THE END?

Of course not—I love writing about Hidden Hollow. My Kindred series is my first love, but immersing myself in a small, magical town where it's almost always Autumn is a nice change of pace. And magic is so much fun to write about—literally anything can happen. I know I promised you Hidden Hollow 2, about the Gargoyle/Angel statue and I do intend to get to it soon. But this is just a fun little adventure in between the main books. Also, if you haven't read the first book in this series, *Sworn to the Orc*, what are you waiting for? Go get it now!

But first, if you have enjoyed *Dreaming of the Demon*, please take a moment to leave a review. Good reviews mean so much and they're an easy way to support your favorite authors and let other readers know it's all right to take a chance on a new series. They also help an author stand out in this crazy book market which is incredibly crowded right now both with human authors and with fake books written by AI. So please leave a review or like a review—I would really appreciate it.

Thank you for being such an awesome reader!

Hugs and Happy Reading to your all,

Evangeline (September 2024)

GIVE A HOT KINDRED WARRIOR TO A FRIEND!

Do you love the Kindred? Do you want to talk about wishing you could go live on the Mother Ship without your friends thinking you're crazy? Well, now it's super easy to get them into the Kindred universe.

Just share this link, **https://bookhip.com/HLNPTP**, with them to download *Claimed*, the first book in my Brides of the Kindred series for FREE.

No strings attached—I don't even want to collect their email for my newsletter. I just want you to be able to share the Kindred world with your besties and have fun doing it.

Hugs and Happy Reading!

Evangeline

SIGN UP FOR MY NEWSLETTER!

Sign up for my newsletter and you'll be the first to know when a new book comes out or I have some cool stuff to give away.

www.evangelineanderson.com/newsletter

Don't worry—I won't share your email with anyone else, I'll never spam you (way too busy writing books) and you can unsubscribe at any time.

As a thank-you gift you'll get a free copy of BONDING WITH THE BEAST delivered to your inbox right away. In the next days I'll also send you free copies of CLAIMED, book 1 in the Brides of Kindred series, and ABDUCTED, the first book in my Alien Mate Index series.

DO YOU LOVE AUDIOBOOKS?

You've read the book, now listen to the audiobook.

My Kindred series is coming to audio one book at a time.
Sign up for my audiobook newsletter below.

www.evangelineanderson.com/audio-newsletter

Besides notifications about new audio releases you may also get an email if I'm running a contest with an audio-book prize. Otherwise I will leave you alone. :).

BECOME A VIP!

The Aliens & Alphas Bookstore offers you exclusive (pre-)releases, special box sets, and reissues of old favorites that you can't find anywhere else.

www.shop.evangelineanderson.com

Sign up for the Aliens & Alphas VIP list to never miss a release, get exclusive sneak peeks, discounts and so much more.

www.shop.evangelineanderson.com/vip-list

ALSO BY EVANGELINE ANDERSON

Below you'll find a list of available and upcoming titles. But depending on when you read this list, new books will have come out by then that are not listed here. Make sure to check my website, www.evangelineanderson.com, for the latest releases and better yet, sign up for my newsletter (www.evangeline-anderson.com/newsletter) to never miss a new book again.

Brides of the Kindred series

(Sci-Fi / Action-Adventure Romance)

CLAIMED*

HUNTED*

SOUGHT*

FOUND*

REVEALED*

PURSUED*

EXILED*

SHADOWED*

CHAINED*

DIVIDED*

DEVOURED*

ENHANCED*

CURSED*

ENSLAVED*

TARGETED*

FORGOTTEN*

SWITCHED*

UNCHARTED*

UNBOUND*

SURRENDERED*

VANISHED*

IMPRISONED*

TWISTED*

DECEIVED*

STOLEN*

COMMITTED*

PUNISHED*

PIERCED*

TRAPPED*

RESCUED*

UNWRAPPED

BRIDES OF THE KINDRED VOLUME ONE

Contains *Claimed, Hunted, Sought* and *Found*

BRIDES OF THE KINDRED VOLUME TWO

Contains *Revealed, Pursued* and *Exiled*

BRIDES OF THE KINDRED VOLUME THREE

Contains *Shadowed, Chained* and *Divided*

BRIDES OF THE KINDRED VOLUME FOUR

Contains *Devoured, Enhanced* and *Cursed*

BRIDES OF THE KINDRED VOLUME FIVE

Contains *Enslaved, Targeted* and *Forgotten*

BRIDES OF THE KINDRED VOLUME SIX

Contains *Switched, Uncharted* and *Unbound*

BRIDES OF THE KINDRED VOLUME SEVEN

Contains *Surrendered, Vanished,* and *Imprisoned*

BRIDES OF THE KINDRED VOLUME EIGHT

Contains *Twisted, Deceived,* and *Stolen*

Also Available in Audio

All Kindred novels are now available in PRINT.

Also, all Kindred novels are on their way to Audio, join my Audiobook Newsletter (www.evangelineanderson.com/audio-newsletter) to be notified when they come out.

Kindred Tales

The Kindred Tales are side stories in the Brides of the Kindred series which stand alone outside the main story arc.

These can be read as STAND ALONE novels.

MASTERING THE MISTRESS*

BONDING WITH THE BEAST*

SEEING WITH THE HEART*

FREEING THE PRISONER*

HEALING THE BROKEN* *(a Kindred Christmas novel)*

TAMING THE GIANT*

BRIDGING THE DISTANCE*

DELIVERED BY THE DEFENDER*

ACCIDENTAL ACQUISITION*

BURNING FOR LOVE*

HIDDEN RAGE*

ENTICED BY THE SATYR*

SAVED BY THE BEAST*

LOVED BY THE LION*

BONDED BY TWO*

TAMING THE TIGER*

DRAGON IN THE DARK*

GUARDED BY THE HYBRID*

QUEEN OF THEIR COLONY*

FINDING HIS GODDESS*

FAKING IT WITH THE HYBRID*

TIED TO THE WULVEN*

SHARED BY THE MONSTRUM*

LOST ON OBLIVION*

WICKED AND WILD

DAE'MONS AND DOMS

KINDRED TALES VOLUME 1

Contains *Mastering the Mistress, Bonding with the Beast* and *Seeing with the Heart*

KINDRED TALES VOLUME 2

Contains *Freeing the Prisoner, Healing the Broken* and *Taming the Giant*

KINDRED TALES VOLUME 3

Contains *Bridging the Distance, Loving a Stranger* and *Finding the Jewel*

KINDRED TALES VOLUME 4

Contains *Bonded by Accident, Releasing the Dragon,* and *Sharing a Mate*

KINDRED TALES VOLUME 5

Contains *Instructing the Novice, Awakened by the Giant,* and *Hitting the Target*

KINDRED TALES VOLUME 6

Contains *Handling the Hybrid, Trapped in Time,* and *Time to Heal*

KINDRED TALES VOLUME 7

Contains *Pairing with the Protector, Falling for Kindred Claus,* and *Guarding the Goddess*

Also Available in Audio

———

Kindle Birthright series

(Sci-Fi / Action-Adventure Romance)

The Children of the Kindred series

UNBONDABLE*

———

Born to Darkness series

(Paranormal / Action-Adventure Romance)

CRIMSON DEBT*

SCARLET HEAT*

RUBY SHADOWS*

CARDINAL SINS (coming soon)

DESSERT* (short novella following *Scarlet Heat*)

BORN TO DARKNESS BOX SET

Contains *Crimson Debt, Scarlet Heat,* and *Ruby Shadows* all in one volume

---

Alien Mate Index series

(Sci-Fi / Action-Adventure Romance)

ABDUCTED*

PROTECTED*

DESCENDED*

SEVERED*

THE OVERLORD'S PET*

THE BARON'S BRIDE*

ALIEN MATE INDEX VOLUME ONE

Contains *Abducted, Protected, Descended* and *Severed* all in one volume

*Also Available in Audio

All Alien Mate novels are now available in PRINT.

The Cougarville series

(Paranormal / Action-Adventure Romance)

(Older Woman / Younger Man

BUCK NAKED*

COUGAR BAIT*

STONE COLD FOX*

BIG, BAD WOLF*

*Also Available in Audio

The CyBRG Files with Mina Carter

(Sci-Fi / Action-Adventure Romance)

UNIT 77: BROKEN*

UNIT 78: RESCUED*

*Also Available in Audio

The Institute series

(Daddy-Dom / Age Play Romance)

THE INSTITUTE: DADDY ISSUES*

THE INSTITUTE: MISHKA'S SPANKING*

*Also Available in Audio

The Swann Sister Chronicles

(Contemporary Fairy / Funny / Fantasy Romance)

WISHFUL THINKING*

BE CAREFUL WHAT YOU WISH FOR*

*Also Available in Audio

Nocturne Academy

(Young Adult Paranormal/Action-Adventure/Romance)

LOCK AND KEY*

FANG AND CLAW*

STONE AND SECRET*

Also Available in Audio

Detectives Valenti and O'Brian

(1980s M/M Romance)

THE ASSIGNMENT

I'LL BE HOT FOR CHRISTMAS

FIREWORKS

THE ASSIGNMENT: HEART AND SOUL

Forbidden Omegaverse Series

(Paranormal Romance

Step-Brother / Foster Brother Romance)

HIS OMEGA'S KEEPER*

THE BRAND THAT BINDS*

HEAT CYCLE*

SINS OF THE FLESH*

FORBIDDEN DESIRE

Also Available in Audio

Hidden Hollow

(Spicy Monster Romance)

SWORN TO THE ORC*

DREAMING OF THE DEMON

The Shadow Fae

(Dark Fantasy Romance)

THE THRONE OF SHADOWS*

THE QUEEN OF MIDNIGHT

Compendiums and Box Sets

ALIEN MATE INDEX VOLUME ONE

Contains *Abducted, Protected, Descended* and *Severed* all in one volume

BORN TO DARKNESS BOX SET

Contains *Crimson Debt, Scarlet Heat*, and *Ruby Shadows* all in one volume

BRIDES OF THE KINDRED VOLUME ONE

Contains *Claimed, Hunted, Sought* and *Found*

BRIDES OF THE KINDRED VOLUME TWO

Contains *Revealed, Pursued* and *Exiled*

BRIDES OF THE KINDRED VOLUME THREE

Contains *Shadowed, Chained* and *Divided*

BRIDES OF THE KINDRED VOLUME FOUR

Contains *Devoured, Enhanced* and *Cursed*

BRIDES OF THE KINDRED VOLUME FIVE

Contains *Enslaved, Targeted* and *Forgotten*

BRIDES OF THE KINDRED VOLUME SIX

Contains *Switched, Uncharted* and *Unbound*

BRIDES OF THE KINDRED VOLUME SEVEN

Contains *Surrendered, Vanished,* and *Imprisoned*

BRIDES OF THE KINDRED VOLUME EIGHT

Contains *Twisted, Deceived,* and *Stolen*

HAVE YOURSELF A SEXY LITTLE CHRISTMAS

Contains *Kidnapped for Christmas, Cougar Christmas* and *Season's Spankings*

KINDRED TALES VOLUME 1

Contains *Mastering the Mistress, Bonding with the Beast* and *Seeing with the Heart*

KINDRED TALES VOLUME 2

Contains *Freeing the Prisoner, Healing the Broken* and *Taming the Giant*

KINDRED TALES VOLUME 3

Contains *Bridging the Distance, Loving a Stranger* and *Finding the Jewel*

KINDRED TALES VOLUME 4

Contains *Bonded by Accident, Releasing the Dragon,* and *Sharing a Mate*

KINDRED TALES VOLUME 5

Contains *Instructing the Novice, Awakened by the Giant,* and *Hitting the Target*

KINDRED TALES VOLUME 6

Contains *Handling the Hybrid, Trapped in Time,* and *Time to Heal*

KINDRED TALES VOLUME 7

Contains *Pairing with the Protector, Falling for Kindred Claus,* and *Guarding the Goddess*

NAUGHTY TALES: THE COLLECTION— Volume One

Contains *Putting on a Show, Willing Submission, The Institute: Daddy Issues, The Institute: Mishka's Spanking, Confessions of a Lingerie Model, Sin Eater, Speeding Ticket, Stress Relief* and *When Mr. Black Comes Home.*

ONE HOT HALLOWEEN

Contains *Red and the Wolf, Gypsy Moon* and *Taming the Beast*

ONE HOT HALLOWEEN Vol.2

Contains *The Covenant, Secret Thirst,* and *Kristen's Addiction* + BONUS: *Madeline's Mates*

Stand Alone Titles

(Sci-Fi OR Paranormal Action-Adventure Romance)

ANYONE U WANT

BEST KEPT SECRETS (Step-Brother romance)

BLIND DATE WITH A VAMPIRE

BLOOD KISS

BROKEN BOUNDARIES (M/M romance)

CEREMONY OF THREE

COMPANION 3000*

DEAL WITH THE DEVIL*

DEFILED

EYES LIKE A WOLF (Foster Brother romance)

FOREVER BROKEN (M/M romance)

GYPSY MOON

HIS OMEGA'S KEEPER* (Step-Brother romance)

HUNGER MOON RISING

MADELINE'S MATES

MARKED

OUTCAST

PLANET X*

PLEASURE PLANET

PLEDGE SLAVE (M/M romance)

PUNISHING TABITHA

PURITY*

RED AND THE WOLF*

SECRET THIRST

SEX WITH STRANGERS

SHADOW DREAMS

SLAVE BOY (M/M romance)

STRESS RELIEF

SWEET DREAMS

TAMING THE BEAST

TANDEM UNIT

THE BARGAIN*

THE COVENANT*

THE LAST BITE (M/M romance)

THE LAST MAN ON EARTH*

THE LOST BOOKS (M/M romance)

THE PLEASURE PALACE

THE SACRIFICE*

THE THRONE OF SHADOWS

'TIL KINGDOM COME (M/M romance)

*Also Available in Audio

Stand Alone Titles

(Contemporay Romance)

A SPANKING FOR VALENTINE (BDSM)

BOUND AND DETERMINED, anthology with Lena Matthews, includes

The Institute: Mishka's Spanking, Confessions of a Lingerie Model, Sin Eater, Speeding Ticket, Stress Relief and *When Mr. Black Comes Home.*

YA Novels

THE ACADEMY*

Also Available in Audio

ABOUT THE AUTHOR

Evangeline Anderson is the *New York Times* and *USA Today* bestselling author of the *Brides of the Kindred, Alien Mate Index, Cougarville,* and *Born to Darkness* series. She lives in Florida with a husband, a son, and the voices in her head. (Mostly characters who won't shut up.) She has been writing sci-fi and paranormal romance for years and she welcomes reader comments and suggestions at
www.evangelineanderson.com.

Or, to be the first to find out about new books, join her newsletter:
www.evangelineanderson.com/newsletter

For updates on Young Adult releases only sign up here instead:
www.evangelineanderson.com/young-adult-newsletter

She's also got a mailing list for updates on audio books:
www.evangelineanderson.com/audio-newsletter

f facebook.com/evangelineandersonauthorpage

X x.com/EvangelineA

instagram.com/evangeline_anderson_author

pinterest.com/vangiekitty

g goodreads.com/evangelineanderson

BB bookbub.com/authors/evangeline-anderson

tiktok.com/@evangelineanderson

www.ingramcontent.com/pod-product-compliance
Ingram Content Group UK Ltd.
Pitfield, Milton Keynes, MK11 3LW, UK
UKHW021422020425
5285UKWH00029B/268

9 798339 649595